I0666203

BATES TRAINING CENTER

First Edition

Published by The Nazca Plains Corporation
Las Vegas, Nevada
2009

ISBN: 978-1-935509-59-2

Published by

The Nazca Plains Corporation ®
4640 Paradise Rd, Suite 141
Las Vegas NV 89109-8000

PUBLISHER'S NOTE
Bates Training Center is a work of fiction created wholly by *Bill Smith*'s imagination. All characters are fictional and any resemblance to any persons living or deceased is purely by accident. No portion of this book reflects any real person or events.

Cover Photos, Konradbak and Imagine
Art Director, Blake Stephens

BATES TRAINING CENTER

First Edition

Bill Smith

It was the first time I had ever been in a lawyer's office. The letter had arrived only three days ago informing me I needed to meet with a Mr. Ashcroft Lindsley, owner of the local prestigious law firm bearing his name. The letter only stated "concerning the matter of your great-uncle's estate." I was aware my great-uncle had died recently, but I had only met the aged man twice in my life and could barely remember what he looked like at this point, let alone what he did for a living although I was well aware he was a community leader and highly respected throughout the Pittsburgh community. After receiving the letter, I phoned the law office immediately, talked to an extremely polite male secretary, and scheduled an appointment with Mr. Lindsley.

I arrived at the elegant law office exactly as scheduled and was promptly shown into Mr. Lindsley's plush office by the secretary and introduced with my full name, Jonathan Randolph Bates. The secretary was worth the visit alone. He was a slave, of course, as was most office help these days. His tightly fitted collar, though, was a tasteful, but expensive, silver. It was 3" tall which forced his handsome head into a constant upright position, making sure you could appreciate his deep blue eyes, his long black eyelashes, his high cheekbones, and his thick, fine black hair tastefully cut in a short Marine-style which emphasized his rugged jawbone and overall masculinity. Below his collar, he wore a skin-tight light blue T-shirt which displayed his well defined pecs and abs along with the firm's logo and below that he had been squeezed into a pair of light blue tights similar to a ballet dancer which fully exhibited his muscular bubble butt and every detail of his huge basket, more so than if he had been naked. His feet were shod in the latest fashion: slip-ons made out of tanned jet black slave hide. As the slave secretary served me coffee during the brief wait for Mr. Lindsley, I could study the slave's physique thoroughly, including his genitals which obviously swelled as he became aware I was inspecting all aspects of his body with my eyes. He lifted his eyes briefly for full eye contact, letting me know in that quick moment that he was pleased I found him worth looking at and he was available if his master so allowed.

"What a whore," I thought to myself, but quickly checked myself in evaluating his motives. After all, slaves had no choice in either their sexual preferences or activities and simply did what they were instructed. At least, that's what all my friends' slaves did - the only slaves I had really paid much attention to one way or the other.

"Why is it I'm so damn poor I can't even afford one runty slave, let alone something like the magnificent piece of meat flaunting himself in front of me in an outfit that seemed more revealing than if he had been butt-naked?" I pondered silently as the slave's pleasant scent of sandalwood reached me in stooping over to refill my coffee cup. His swollen genitals were once again practically thrust in my face as he assumed a stance right in front of me with a big smile before returning to his desk. If I owned something like that, I'd have those clothes off of him and have him bent over that desk of his for the best fucking of his life before the slave would even know what had happened. Lost in the reverie of the moment, I imagined what it would be like to thrust deeply into the 'boy' (all slaves, regardless of age, were referred to as 'boy' to denote their dependent status) and hear him moan as I pumped deeply into him.

Then strangely, I wondered how the slave felt being paraded around like this, obviously available for whichever client Mr. Lindsley "gave" him to that particular day. Was he embarrassed or was he long past that? Did he begrudge his status, or had he learned to actually enjoy being desired and wanted? Did he resent being fucked or whatever whenever his master decided, having no choice of with whom or what he would be doing, or did it matter anymore? Is it possible he had learned to accept his fate and actually enjoyed having a life well-ordered, reasonably secure, with no concerns about getting enough to eat, having a roof over his head, getting fired, getting laid, or not being able to pay all his bills - all concerns I had to face each and every day. Was it possible that slaves actually were the ones better off in the long haul despite having their hides turned into shoe leather upon their death?

My reverie ended with the secretary politely escorting me into Mr. Lindsley's plush office and introducing me using my full formal name.

"Jonathan Randolph Bates, Master," the slave said humbly as he assumed a kneeling position by the side of the desk, keeping his eyes on the floor in front of him, but spreading his knees wide to fully expose his beautifully displayed basket.

"How good of you to come in so quickly, Mr. Bates. I assume my slave here has offered you coffee and anything else that might add to your comfort?" Mr. Lindsley started out, with a knowing look at the end of his last statement. "The slave has earned quite a reputation in seeing to my client's personal comforts," he added as he reached down and ran his hand through the slave's hair, similar to patting a dog. "He rarely gets a chance to serve a client as young as yourself and I'm sure he would delight in the novelty of servicing you compared to his usual obligations. Isn't that right, Pleasure?"

"Yes indeed, Master," the slave answered, looking up quickly at his master and unconsciously running his tongue across his lips. "I would love to service the young client if you want me to, Master." Pleasure's voice was deep, humble, soft and, surprisingly, sounded totally sincere. I was unaware such good looking slaves could be trained to that level but then, I really knew very little about slaves or the training they had prior to being placed into service.

"Pleasure is from right here in Pittsburgh, Mr. Bates, in case you were wondering."

I wasn't, but found the information interesting.

"He was sold by the Allegheny Crime Commission shortly after his trial - a 19-year-old drug runner in the slums. After a good year of training, the firm bought him for the office staff and I've had him almost as soon as he arrived here from the sales barn. He's a good secretary and almost all my clients appreciate his other talents. We frequently sent him out on overnight or even weekend loans to clients who throw a lot of business our way. He comes back a little tired looking but I've never heard a complaint." He again reached down to the slave's face, lifted his chin up and inserted a finger into the slave's mouth who promptly began vigorously sucking on the inserted finger. "See, even now, he's eager to go. Damn well trained if I do say so myself which gets to why I asked you here today."

"I was wondering..." I drifted off as the slave keep nosily slurping on Mr. Lindsley's middle finger, now thrust all the way down the slave's throat.

"Well, Pleasure here was trained at Bates Slave Training Center - surely, you've heard of it?"

"Sure, who hasn't?" I responded, wondering what the most respected and by far the largest training facility in the city had to do with my being in Mr. Lindsley's office.

"Haven't you ever wondered about the name - Bates?"

"I lot of people carry that name, Mr. Lindsley."

"That's true, but in this case your family name of Bates and the Bates Training Center are directly connected," Mr. Lindsley continued with a sense of delicious irony in his voice. "Your great uncle, Randolph Bates, owned and operated Bates Training Center part and parcel. He was the biggest and probably best slave trainer in this entire region. At least most people thought so. Bates' products are coveted throughout the United States and most people are willing to pay huge premiums to own a Bates' trained slave."

"I know the reputation, Mr. Lindsley - who hasn't? But I never associated my great-uncle as that Bates! He always seemed so quiet and unassuming. The thought never crossed my mind that Uncle Randolph had any money or anything, let alone be an esteemed slave trainer."

"Well, he was. And his reputation was well earned. Look at this 'boy' kneeling in front of us sucking my finger like his life depended on it. He's a product of your great-uncle's well-regarded training techniques. If Pleasure here is like all the other Bates' trained slaves I know of, he'll stay just as good a slave 50 years from now as he is now. That's what your great-uncle produced: slave training that lasted a lifetime. Add to that the fact Bates' Training only picked the best stock to start with and that meant you got a very handsome, muscular, well hung and always cooperative and willing slave for the considerable dollars they cost. This 'boy' here is a perfect example: he's about as good looking as they come, he's always cooperative and interested in doing what you want the best he can, and, as you can see through his tights, he's about as well equipped as slaveboys get, even those specially bred for the market as out and out sex slaves. Incidentally, Bates' Training not only trained bred slaves as well as acquired slaves, but your great-uncle was spearheading a drive to set up their own breeding facilities at the time of his unfortunate death."

"He was always so quiet and unpretentious when I met him. I never imagined he had any money, let alone a reputation as one of Pittsburgh's outstanding entrepreneurs and a leader in slave training. He never said a word about it - at least to me. But why would he? I wasn't anything to him probably - just a poor boy struggling to feed his face down in the low-rent district."

"Don't run yourself down, Mr. Bates. Your great-uncle apparently saw right through that facade and, although he could have easily left his estate to charity, left it entirely to you as his only living relative. I mistakenly assumed you already knew you were your great-uncle's only heir, Mr. Bates. He left everything, his entire estate, to you."

"You're kidding," I stared at him. "I can't even remember what he looked like and he barely knew me at all."

"Well, he knew you were his only living relative," Mr. Lindsley smiled.

"Without appearing crude, did he actually have much of an 'estate'?" I asked with obvious discomfort. "I've heard of Bates Training, of course, but does that amount to much?"

"Indeed it does," Mr. Lindsley said. "Considerable."

I sat in shock for a long while trying to digest this momentous bit of good news while Mr. Lindsley passed the time playing with the slave kneeling beside him, now ordered to quickly strip out of his tight fitting clothes so he was totally nude before his master. Mr. Lindsley lost no time in fondling his slave's tits until they were swollen and erect, running his hands all over his well muscled body, and finally, stroking the slave's rigid penis until it was fully erect and dripping. When I still didn't respond to the news, Mr. Lindsley calmly pumped the slave until the slave's body stiffened and a full load of steamy hot cum was delivered into Mr. Lindsley's well manicured hands. Mr. Lindsley took his time licking the cum off his hands bit by bit, obviously enjoying this afternoon snack, before ordering the slave to don his outfit once again. I overheard the attractive slave thank his master humbly as he was struggling back into the skin-tight clothes, just what for I couldn't figure out. Finally, I spoke.

"Mr. Lindsley, I know nothing about training slaves - hell, I don't even own one - never could afford even an old broken down one, let alone a product of Bates' Training where even I know only the best are processed."

"Don't worry, John. The trainers in place, all slaves owned by your uncle, are well versed in how to run the place and your uncle left full instructions. There's a lot of ins and outs to the business, I understand, but he stated in his will that he was fully confident that you could manage it quite well upon his death."

I continued to stare at him in disbelief.

"Your great-uncle Randolph has left you an estate of over 36 million dollars, mainly in slave stock on hand and a magnificent training facility right here in Pittsburgh. The estate includes 80 highly experienced trainers, all Mr. Bates' personal slaves themselves, as well as 312 premium slaves in various stages of training, including 45 completely trained and ready for immediate sale. That's not including his beautiful manor house in downtown Pittsburgh completely staffed by slaves, including six male pleasure slaves Mr. Bates kept for his personal use. I assume you knew your uncle was never attracted to females in any way, even to the point of leaving no immediate heirs. But he was certainly known about town for his taste in beautiful male slaveboys and made no secret of the fact he used them frequently within the privacy of his own home. In fact," Mr. Lindsley chucked, "his friends often referred to him as 'Randy Randolph'. He was only 61 when he died and was still going strong. Frankly," Mr. Lindsley smiled, "he died about as happy as a man can be - fucking one of his pleasure slaves - I understand. They've got the slave he was fucking locked up in a separate cage with Randolph's cum still up his ass until the inquest has been completed so that there is no question that there was no malfeasance in his death. He died as a real man - exerting his authority over this property for his own pleasure. A good end for a man of your great-uncle's stature in the community if I do say myself."

I sat there drinking my now luke-warm coffee mulling the whole situation over. I was well aware of slaves, of course. Everyone was. They were everywhere, doing most of the hard work, keeping the parks clean, attending their mistresses and masters - it was impossible not to notice them. It was common knowledge anyone with two pennies to rub together - which didn't include me - had a slave or two around for his sexual pleasure. But the truth was only about the upper third of the free population could afford even one slave, let alone a whole parcel. That luxury was restricted to the truly wealthy - the upper 5% or so who seemed to have whole squadrons of them around for one thing or another. And most corporations, along with most industrial operations, including almost all construction and maintenance firms, now depended on 100% slave labor to keep operating cost competitive. No one could deny we lived in a slave society, especially now that it was estimated about 65% of the total population were slaves - either born into it or enslaved since birth on one legal pretext or another. And all those slaves, especially those recently enslaved, had to be trained to their new status. That's where facilities like my great-uncle's were essential in the society. Everyone knew they were needed, highly profitable, and appreciated for the quality of their output. Being a slave trainer was a highly esteemed position in society, even higher than a slave dealer. Both professions offered essential and needed services, offering services that were the "oil" that kept the society running smoothly: supplying highly trained and well conditioned slaves where they were needed and where they would serve with a minimum amount of disciplining and supervision. I knew the Bates Slave Training Center was highly respected for the quality of the training it provided. The center had the reputation of turning even the most rebellious newly enslaved rogue into a compliant useful servant for life no matter what the slave was called upon to perform in his new life. True, Bates slaves were expensive to buy, but they only trained the best of the lot and their training techniques seemed to last the slave's life. It was money well spent when you bought a 'Bates slave'.

Mr. Lindsley was still enjoying his afternoon snack of hot slave cum on his fingers while he gave me time to absorb all that he had said. Finally, he stood up and led me to a small door from his office I hadn't noted before because it seemed to be part of his wall-to-wall bookcase. Swinging back a section of the bookcase, he led me through the hidden entrance.

"I thought you might like to see one of your great-uncle's properties I had moved to a holding cell I have right here close to my office. I usually keep one of my own slaves in the cell for use by some of my clients who prefer something different from my secretary, but today I had the slave your great-uncle was fucking when he died transferred here for the convenience of the inquest and so you could see one of your newly acquired properties up close and personal so to speak. You know, John, you're going to have to get use to inspecting a lot of your new properties and here you can begin the process in total privacy. Besides, I thought you would find interesting just exactly the type of slave your Great-Uncle Randolph enjoyed bedding down."

Just on the other side of the door was a small cell holding one of the six slaves my Great-Uncle kept for his personal pleasure.

"This slave was one of your Uncle Randolph's favorites, Jonathan. I know because I was one of your Uncle's close friends and he often loaned me the use of his personal slaves. I've enjoyed this 'boy' many times myself, but no one will fuck him until the inquest is over and your uncle's cum has been extracted from his ass to verify exactly how he died and when. You can tell the exact age of cum as long as it's kept nice and warm like in a boy's ass," he added casually.

I looked over the young slaveboy (actually a young man in his early twenties but all slaves were referred to as 'boy'), chained by his wrists and ankles to manacles in the holding cell for full display. The slave looked terror struck, not knowing what was going to happen to him. Would he be put to death for 'causing' his former owner's demise in the excitement of fucking him, sold off quickly to an out-of-town buyer to avoid any embarrassment to his former owner's heirs, or sent back to the Training Center that had produced him for retraining as an anonymous draft slave and then sold off at the next auction.

He was still fresh looking despite all the experience my uncle had no doubt put him through and, despite his pensiveness as to his unpredictable fate at this point, was still extremely sexy. His blond hair, brilliant blue eyes, pouting lips, magnificent musculature, creamy, hairless body, strikingly handsome face, and well-shaped exceptionally large sexual organs (even now fully erect and dripping) was practically the epitome of masculinity in a young, appealing body. I felt myself getting hard just looking at the slave and wondered what it would be like to pound the 'boy's' ass myself or have him on his knees sucking me off. There was little doubt as to why the 'boy' had been chosen and then trained as a pleasure slave.

Your great-uncle sure knew how to pick a boy, didn't he?" Mr. Lindsley said, staring pointedly at the arousal clearly visible in my tented pants. "Don't be embarrassed. I've never seen a free man yet who this slave doesn't turn on. Believe me, he's as good in action as he looks. I know - I've bedded him down at least a dozen times over at your great-uncle's estate."

"I wonder where he came from?" I asked innocently enough.

"Right here in Pittsburgh. Your great-uncle bought him at a court sale a couple of years ago. The boy had stolen a pack of cigarettes from a convenience store as I recall and you know yourself what the laws are now. The so-called larceny didn't matter according to your late great-uncle. The boy didn't have a pot to pee in anyway - his parents had died in a car accident a few months before his crime and he didn't have any money to live on so he had resorted to selling his body to feed his face. Actually, he's better off as a slave than he was hustling out on the streets - better fed and cared for anyway," Mr. Lindsley said convincingly. "Without that nice body he would have starved to death long ago and this slave knows it" he added as he reached down and stroked the boy's prick whereupon it quickly became fully erect and started to drip. "Knowing what your assets are is half the battle in a slave selling himself on the open market. John, after you've had a chance to use this 'boy' yourself to your complete satisfaction, you can put this slave up on the auction block for sale and I would judge you'll get at least $1 million for him, maybe more if you body shave him and get him properly collared, tit-ringed and a good cinch fitted to show off his package. You might even consider nose-ringing him - it's quite the fashion nowadays. My friends tell me a lot of masters are having their pleasure slaves fitted with one currently. If you decide to sell him, I may buy him myself," Mr. Lindsley chuckled as he continued to stroke the slave, "but I'd definitely give him a full body shave and get him properly ringed."

"Your uncle was strange when it came to his personal bed bucks. He liked them 'au natural' as he called it - no body shaves, no rings or bands fitted on them, not even a proper slave collar. Hell, he even kept a full bush on them for some unknown reason. Not collaring the slave is against the law as you know, Jonathan, but your uncle insisted it wasn't necessary in that they would never leave his manor house anyway and he loved seeing all of their neck muscles when he was fucking them. He even left the hair around their assholes. Claimed the hair held the lube in them better after they were flushed. Crazy stuff like that! Doesn't matter now though, does it? I'm sure he'll be shaved and fitted completely before he's ever put back on the marketplace. Well trained white boys like this are bringing top dollar now, John. Look, he's dripping steady already just from us talking about him - that's the sort of thing buyers like when they're looking to purchase a new boy for their bed."

My eyes were fixated on the slave's dripping erection and I was transfixed by the overall beauty of the slave's body. I couldn't imagine what it might be like to have such a boy at my complete disposal as, apparently, my great-uncle did each and every day. I couldn't remember ever seeing a slave this attractive, but then, of course, I rarely saw slaves at all in my miserable existence and the ones I did see were the cheap, low quality draft slaves cleaning up the garbage or unloading delivery trucks. Their often naked bodies were usually so ugly, you diverted your eyes when you came upon them. It was a blessing when their owners gave the ugliest ones a few rags to cover themselves, thereby sparing the free citizens forced to look at them when they weren't in their "kennels."

"I've made sure my day was free for your visit, John, in that I was sure you would want to visit the source of your new-found wealth."

"Well, Mr. Lindsley, I suppose I should," I said still in shock. "But, as I said, I know nothing about slave training at this point and I'm not sure I would know what to look for," I apologized.

"You don't need to know anything yet, John. The trainers in place there now, all long-time slaves of your uncle, know their trade very well and will be glad to explain any of their procedures you're interested in. I can give you a general overview in that your great-uncle and I shared many things over the years, including his concerns about the slave training business and where it was headed. That's why he entrusted his will to me. Besides, if the general manager is in, he can tell you anything you want - his knowledge in the area of slave training is encyclopedic."

"Well, if you overlook my naiveté in all this, I'll take you up on your kind offer. That is, if you feel you can spare the time," I smiled for the first time at Mr. Lindsley.

"Spare the time? Your great-uncle paid me well, John, including making sure the will's terms were met. Meaning of course, that he wanted YOU to take over and run Bates Training."

"It's still hard to believe, but I suppose we should get started," was all I could say. "I've got to start somewhere and now's probably a good a time as any."

"That's the spirit, John," Mr. Lindsley said enthusiastically. Without hesitation, we returned to his office, he ordered the kneeling slave Pleasure back to his desk, and led me down to the parking lot to his brand new luxury car. We quickly headed to Bates Training, only a couple of miles from the law office.

"We'll look at your great-uncle's manor house later, John," Mr. Lindsey said as the powerful car sped to its destination. "Wait till you see the staff there at the house. Your Great-Uncle Randolph liked having the best looking slaves available around him at all times and his personal pleasure slaves are all as good looking as that young boy back in the little holding cell off my office."

When we approached Bates Training, the first thing noticeable was a handsome male slave chained to a podium right outside the entrance advertising the wares to be had inside. The slave, looking to be in his early 20s, was held in place by a short leash attached to the end of his sizeable penis. His body was totally shaved with the exception of the dark thick hair atop his head while a heavy collar, arm bands, a body harness, and low boots gave him a totally controlled look. He was semi-erect even now exposed to the world at large and smiled brightly as we approached the front entrance. Mr. Lindsley informed me he was an imported German slave and, now that he was fully trained, would fetch close to $1.2 million when auctioned.

"Buy me, masters. You won't be disappointed, masters," he pleaded politely in a soft voice as we approached the front entrance. "I will do everything to please a new master," he added.

"This is your new master, slave," Mr. Lindsley said harshly. "He just inherited you."

The German slave promptly fell to his knees and touched his forehead to the ground in full slave obeisance.

"Display," Mr. Lindsley ordered and the slave immediately put his hands in back of his neck, rose full height and thrust his pelvis out as he spread his legs far apart.

Mr. Lindsley hefted the slave's balls and then stroked the slave's ringed penis until it was fully erect and the chain leash was pulled into suspension. "Assume your sitting position, slave," Mr. Lindsley ordered as he released the slave's sexual organs. "We don't have time to fuck you now."

"Yes, master," the slave replied humbly as he again sat down at the entrance with his knees spread wide to fully display his sexual organ. But he glanced admiringly at the young Mr. Bates, making sure his new owner knew he would be happy to service him at any time.

"Randolph's agent found this slave for sale in Istanbul. He had been highjacked from a bar there when he drunk a beer with some knock-out drops in it. Before his capture by the Turkish slavers, he had been a sailor onboard a German freighter knocking about the Mediterranean. But when the barman found out he had no family and had just been fired from the freighter, he called his slaver friends who had him naked and caged by the time the knock-out drops wore off. Within a day, he had been sold to your uncle's agent and the next thing he knew his cage was being unloaded here in Pittsburgh where his training began. It all turned out quite well, didn't it?" Mr. Lindsley said giving the slave a final look as we entered the front entrance of the training establishment.

"John, let me give you an overview of the training procedures before we go into any detail. That way, you'll know what questions to ask."

"Sounds good to me, Mr. Lindsley. It's hard for me to believe I actually own that handsome slave exposing himself there at the doorway."

"Well, you do, John, and hundreds more just as good looking and appealing as that piece of meat," Mr. Lindsley said. "Get used to it!"

With that, we entered the facility itself and a whole new world was opened to me. Unexpectedly, I found myself erect and dripping during the entire tour as I looked over all the new "property" I had just inherited.

"Here's where the new stock arrives," Mr. Lindsley said as we looked at a white slave short-chained to a loading pallet which could be handled by a fork-lift. The slave was muzzled, collared, and chained in such a position that he could not move from his kneeling position. He was obviously muscular but nothing probably like he would be after some heavy forced exercise routines imposed on almost all slaves in training prior to their sale.

"When he's released, he won't be able to walk for several hours due to the cramping caused by the short-chaining, but he's already learned he's not in charge anymore. That's important as a first lesson for any slave. This particular slave isn't much, really - probably Class C, but he's worth training in that he's young enough to get a lot of use out of him over a lifetime."

The slave was a little old, but one could see that once shaved, cleaned, and fully trained for service, he should still bring a good price on the auction block.

"This is a good example of a Class C slave," Mr. Lindlsey said as we stopped by the pallet holding the chained shave. "He doesn't reek of youthful vigor; he isn't strikingly good looking, his body isn't breathtakingly muscular or well defined, and his sexual organs, although fully adequate, are not colossal. Class C slaves, fully trained to immediate obedience of any and all demands without hesitation, do offer a long life span of service, good value for the investment in their purchase, and can easily be converted to draft slaves once their sexual appeal fades. They generally bring around $300,000 to $400,000 at auction if completely broken to their slavery and fully trained. If training is incomplete, they are sold off in lots as laborers, usually worked in chain gangs under a steady whip - you've probably see the gangs yourself working on the roads and such with a heavy whip biting into their back and rumps fairly steadily to keep them at it. If they end up that way, their only sexual outlet is servicing their overseers who rape them on a regular basis," Mr. Lindsley chuckled, "so they're far better off if they shape up to avoid that plight."

"Where did this one come from?" Mr. Lindsley asked the intake supervisor, himself a Bates Training slave. The slave being discussed couldn't answer. The muzzle strapped around his head would prevent any talk until he was either completely voice-trained or his vocal cords had been snipped, not uncommon in slaves where speech wasn't required in their work.

"England, master," the supervisor slave answered. "Mr. Bates bought him from the prisons over there. He knocked up a rich banker's daughter over there and was charged with statutory rape whereupon the courts sentenced him to slavery for life."

"Stupid, wasn't it?" Mr. Lindsley laughed. "With all the slave girls available in England these days, everyone of whom you can fuck with impunity, why in God's name would he pick a free girl to fuck?"

The slave overseer rolled his eyes in full agreement but otherwise didn't comment. Love wasn't a motive as far as slaves were concerned.

"Well, he's more likely to be fucked himself now than run around fucking someone," Mr. Lindsley laughed. "He'll learn all about that during his training, John. One of a new slave's first lessons, after he's been broken to his new status, is how to suck properly and take a good fucking. For most of them, it's a whole new experience and tells them clearly they are slaves now, put on this earth to bring pleasure to whoever buys them."

As they entered another room, Mr. Lindsley announced that processing slaves is a science now - highly refined and fully perfected. He then introduced me as the new owner of the firm to the head manager, Brett Alcorn.

Mr. Alcorn respectfully showed me the basic procedures new trainees underwent as part of the initial basic training.

"In the first stages of processing a new slave, he or she is taught to cooperate with anything asked of him through the administration of severe electric shocks. The administration of severe pain is an old, but still highly effective training tool," he explained, "especially when it is delivered for no other reason that just because you are now a slave. In fact, a slave learns that pain can be administered anytime for no other reason than it pleases your new owner.

"Next, a new slave's body is completely shaved with the usual exception of his head hair. There's something about taking a man's hair away from him, going clear back to the Old Testament stories about Samson losing his strength when his hair was shirred. Slaves are true to that legend - when you shave off their chest hair, the hair under their arms, and especially the bush surrounding their sexual organs and their asshole, they end up looking like a child in their opinion. That's exactly what we want - they are a 'boy' again just like they will be called from now on. Besides, shaving them bare fully exposes their sex and not only makes it appear much larger, but makes the slave feel totally vulnerable. When we then ring his tits so they're permanently swollen and enlarged, install a tight clinch on his genitals forcing them to protrude out for all to see and feel easily and making them appear much larger, often band his wrists and ankles so restraining chains can be easily attached, and usually even pierce his septum so a nose ring can be installed, at least for training. He definitely can't help but feel exactly like an animal because he associates a nose ring clearly with all the farm animals he's seen up to that point if he'd never been around slaves before. But the heavy metal slave collar does more than anything to teach a slave his new status in the world: it marks him as a slave; he's collared like most other livestock, and it's heavy enough to constantly remind him he's now the property of someone else. It's amazing how these simple procedures teach a new slave his body is no longer his own and changes his whole prospective on his situation.

"Next, painfully loud audio mantras are fed to the trainee around the clock through earphones locked on him along with random administration of electric shocks while he strapped tightly down so he can't move. The mantras include: 'Your body belongs to your master,' 'your body will be used to please your new owner,' 'you must always instantly obey any order given you,' 'you are never to talk unless your master or mistress orders it,' 'you may never touch your sex unless your master orders it,' etc. When the slave screams in agony from the shocks, it's a great time to check out their teeth since their mouth is wide open anyway. Investment in dentures always pays off - buyers are turned off by bad teeth in a new purchase.

"After 48 hours, most slaves are in total shock and are psychologically beginning to accept their new status. They're now 'ready' for the real training to begin. Of course, bred slaves can skip all this and go directly into specialized training. But a captured slave can always be broken to his slavery - it's just a matter of time and knowing the right techniques to employ."

By that time, we were passing a station where naked slaves were again strapped down to tables, obviously in the 'shock' stage the supervisor had described with their eyes distant and their bodies totally tensed. One of the slaves nearest me was magnificent: a young blond with a great build, well defined pecs, a huge prick already semi-erect and drop dead looks. He had the looks most people fantasize about.

The manager saw me looking at the prone boy and could tell I was excited by his looks. "Don't worry, Mr. Bates, we'll have this one fully trained and over in the manor house for you in no time at all if your interest holds," he laughed. "Your great-uncle would have push a 'rush' tag on this boy's training if he were still around. He's just the type, with his looks and equipment, the 'big boss' liked as his personal pleasure slaves," he informed me with no embarrassment in his voice. Prudery wasn't a useful concept in the slave training business apparently.

Overall, Brett Alcorn's explanations were terse, informative, and gave me a good overview of the basic procedures. My 'inherited' manager never talked down to me despite my total ignorance in the area and always managed to convey great respect for my position as the new owner of the enterprise despite my obvious youth. What struck me was how he viewed his work totally objectively, seeing the 'stock' being trained as nothing more or less than livestock being readied for market. When I commented on this, he answered with his characteristic bluntness.

"But that's exactly what they are, Mr. Bates. Livestock."

"Well, yes, Mr. Alcorn. I'm new to all this. Please excuse my naive questions."

"Mr. Bates' great-nephew has never owned slaves until now, Brett. As he'll be the first to tell you, he has a lot to learn," Mr. Lindsley explained.

"Well, Mr. Bates, no matter what they might have been before, they're slaves now and the best thing they can do is learn how to be a slave. That's why we are so proud of our work here at Bates Training. We enable the stock here to live out a useful and happy life in their new circumstances."

By now, we were in a area filled with small cages, each filled with a new 'servant in the making.' Shaved, banded, and evaluated, the caged slaves were being given a break before starting their really serious specialized training. We stopped next to a cage containing a 19-year-old white slave who was well hung, but was too skinny - he needed to build up his musculature considerably during his training in that he was tagged to be trained as a potential pleasure stud.

"If this boy takes to his training well, he should sell for around $800,000 if he reaches Class A Stud levels in his training program,." Brett Alcorn said with enthusiasm. "We'll bulk him out and teach that prick of his some new tricks he never knew anything about."

"They're resting up for evaluation, which is the next room to the left," Brett explained as he led the way into a totally white room filled with bodies strapped face up on examination gurneys. Each slave was surrounded by white robed physicians, psychologists, and nurses all wearing surgical masks and rubber gloves. Totally compliant now, the slaves were being thoroughly examined for general body health, musculature, sexual excitability, and semen output according to Mr. Alcorn. He explained the evaluation team then devised a physical training program to be run simultaneously with their psychological training.

"It's a slave's potential that counts. Any slave can be conditioned into superb musculature and prodigious sexual output if they have the potential presumably spotted by the slave catcher or one of our purchasing agents. But you'll got to have a customized training program to do that efficiently. That's what they're doing here."

We stood by one table as a slave was quickly 'milked' by a nurse to obtain a semen specimen while another nurse took a blood sample from his arm. A doctor was checking the slave's eyes and teeth while they were doing this. Although strapped tightly to the examination table, the slave nevertheless tried to arch his body and gasped as he reached orgasm and a huge load was delivered into an awaiting vial. His face was scarlet in embarrassment at being 'milked' in public with all sorts of onlookers.

"He's a shy one," Brett Alcorn laughed at the slave's flushed body. "He'll get over that soon enough - they all do quickly enough. Personal modesty is totally inappropriate for a body that belongs to someone else now," he stated as if the truism should be self-evident to any slave, even a brand new one.

"Assuming they weren't born into slavery, as apparently this slave wasn't judging from his inappropriate blushing, what are the major events in their training experiences in your opinion as far as accepting their slavery, Brett?" I asked.

"First, Mr. Bates, from their viewpoint, is the experience of being constantly nude which embarrasses them and makes them feel vulnerable. But they get used to that amazingly fast as long as they are around other naked slaves all the time. But when they are forced to be nude when around clothed trainers or potential buyers, they feel like animals - it's the comparison or them being naked and free people being clothed that makes them feel that way. It's a great lesson for slaves to learn - they are just like animals now!

"Second, I suppose, is the installation of the slave collar which is heavy enough to feel it all the time and fixed in place permanently so it marks them as a slave for life. Somehow, they act differently after they're collared - it's a distinction that marks them for what they are - a slave and it's a powerful lesson to them. When you add to that the tit rings, nose rings, ear rings, genitals bands, and all the other slave control devices, they learn their body belongs to someone else now and consequently can be decorated or altered any damn way their new owner desires - just like any other piece of livestock.

Take a nose ring for example. Once that's installed, what's the difference between you and a horse or a boar pig or a cow? You can only imagine what a genital ring does to their thinking. Even their most private parts are now subject to the whims of their owners and can be displayed any way they so please. I've seen new slaves who don't; seem embarrassed by anything we do to them - ring their tits, collar them, even nose ring them. But fasten a tight band around their sexual organs which forces their manhood out for all the world to see and hook a leash on it - even the boldest, brashest slave stops strutting around and begins to realize what being a slave is all about. We generally have a female trainer lead them around on a genital leash after the male trainers have done it, so they get the point they're just property now, not people.

"Third, branding is a life altering experience for most new stock. It's not only a traumatic pain experience, it's also a psychological turning point. Once branded by an owner, you are clearly marked as property - your body is the possession of your mistress or master and the brand with its ownership mark shows the whole world you belong to that person from now on.

"Fourth, again from the slave's viewpoint, is having to stand absolutely still while anyone can feel any part of your body, squeezing it, pinching it, prodding it, stroking it to their heart's content while you just stand there absolutely still. It's a solid admission you now belong to another person and are totally in their control, even if the other person chooses to stroke you to full orgasm right in public, force a baseball bat up your ass, or whip you just for the fun or it. You're nothing but a body to play with and standing on display while a person feels you up to full arousal is a tacit admission you have accepted your master or mistress and his or her total control over your body. We use both female and male trainers for this so a slave gets used to being handled by both.

"Fifth, is taking responsibility for your body's cleanliness. First, we have to strap a slave down to give him his enemas and then watch his humiliation as he empties himself in public. Most free people really cling to their privacy when it comes to shitting. But when he learns he must administer an enema to himself over and over until he runs clean and then lube himself in preparation for being fucked in order to get fed, most new trainees simply can't believe we expect that of them. But after a few forced enemas where he's strapped down and a few days without food for refusing to give themselves enemas, even the most recalcitrant slaves come around and learn to always present themselves to their owners thoroughly cleansed inside and out and with their holes lubed for action. Besides, if you're even been fucked dry, that is without any lube, as most slaves are at some point or another in their early training as an object lesson, a slave will do most anything to earn the privilege of having access to some good lubricant. A dry fucking isn't easily forgotten and takes several days to get over for most of the new slaves.

"When you put it all together, both what is done to them by us, plus their perception of what is happening to them, you can see processing newly captured slaves is a science in itself, just like Mr. Lindsley said earlier."

With that, Brett showed me more of the operation. In the next room were again row after row of stacked cages, each barely able to hold one body. Inside each of them knelt a slave now through with evaluation and awaiting his branding. Each cage held a shivering body with his scrotum now already tightly banded, his tits sore from their recent ringing, and his asshole shaved and open for future usage and with their wrists and ankles chained to the parameters of the cage. The majority, with newly installed nose rings, were fastened to the cage bars with the new device so they couldn't move their head in any way. Each had their ankles chained far apart in the cage so their holes were fully exposed for viewing, a humiliation they now knew would be routine in their lives as slaves. Sweat ran off their trembling bodies as they anticipated being branded with the Bates Training logo on both their left ass check and their right pectoral. After that, they would be clearly and permanently marked as property and every slave in the room knew there would be no going back from their new status now.

I heard stomachs rumbling amongst many of the cages and asked Mr. Alcorn about this.

"New slaves are not fed until 56 hours after processing begins to that they learn their bodily needs are solely dependent on their owners from now on. They've been here about 48 hours now, so they are ravenously hungry and will be fed after they have recovered from their branding. If we fed them before they're branded, they throw it all up anyway from the severe pain and make quite a mess. But after, they can digest it fine. When finally fed, they are ravenously hungry, as you can tell from all the stomach rumbling now, but they must eat their food and water from a bowl on the floor without the use of their hands like any other animal.

Throughout training, they will be fed nothing but a nourishing diet of high protein slave chow designed to build up an excellent musculature and good semen production while keeping them slim and attractive. Overweight slaves are quickly brought down to the rigid specified weight limits by imposing the low calorie version of slave chow as the only alternative to starvation. Unless they are sold to a fairly inexperienced owner, they will be fed twice a day only slave chow from dishes on the floor the rest of their lives - a procedure almost all slave owners follow as a constant reminder that the slave is nothing but livestock now and consequently is fed like livestock.

"Soon after being introduced to the feeding regime, they are introduced to their personal trainer, another slave who specializes in 'breaking' new stock to the demands of the marketplace. The personal trainer has been a slave for years, of course, and has long ago adjusted to being collared, genitally banded, tit ringed, branded, and usually nose ringed. Before the training is over, a strong bond forms between a new slave and his trainer - he identifies with him since they are both slaves and a transference process takes place which helps the new trainee adjust rapidly. One of the hardest things for the trainee to do at this time is adjust to his collar, his rings, and the tight band around his genitals which constantly force them into being displayed and easily accessible. When they see their trainer, similarly banded, is able to disregard the banding and even walks normally with his balls held so high up, he realizes he will adjust also, just as he is already probably getting used to his collar. Just to make sure, the trainers usually thrust their genitals in the trainees face as often as they can to show the new slave it's just part of being a slave. That bond gets so strong over the months of training that the trainees often break down in tears when they are separated from their trainer prior to sale. It's like losing a father to them."

We were passing into the room where slaves, now branded and recuperated, were being given their first meal of slave chow with their hands manacled behind their back, forcing them to eat with their mouth in the bowl like any other livestock would feed. The slaves were having difficulty sucking up the water to alleviate their desperate thirst and using their teeth and tongues to pick up the morsels of dry slave chow which they soon learned to wash down with gulps of the water. The fresh brands were seeping and raw on their butts although we couldn't view their branded pecs well due to their feeding.

"The brands will scar over soon enough," Mr. Alcorn said. "We do a neat job here and within a week it will just leave a nice brown mark, clearly visible to most anyone, marking his new ownership. See how they take to the feeding? Hunger is a powerful motive and can turn even the most sophisticated young man into the livestock he really is soon enough. Slavery is really revealing a boy's true nature to himself, some wag said a few years ago. A lot of truth in that. Slaves are just animals - nothing more, nothing less - but mighty useful once they're trained properly," he added with some pride.

"See this slave here," he pointed to a very handsome slave with his face stuck into the feeding bowl eating as fast as he could without the use of his hands. "He's just turned 20, is mighty good looking when we let him stand upright and show himself, is very well hung if you look down there between his legs, and will develop a good physique with proper diet and exercise. When fully trained, we plan to sell him overseas - with your permission, of course - probably to a Middle Eastern market where his pearly white skin and other attributes will command well over $1 million dollars. Mr. Bates, you're going to find that profits in slaves are enormous if you know the trade well. Most stock is either stolen from the streets at no cost, bought from local jails or state prisons at little cost, like this boy here, or are products of slave breeding farms where they have been reared at minimum cost."

"I looked inside the cage and saw the young man, now totally concentrating on getting food into his gullet at long last, was indeed most appealing from a purely physical viewpoint.

"What will he do once he's sold in the Middle Eastern markets?" I asked.

"Well, any slave worth a million dollars is going to have to earn his keep, believe you me," Mr. Alcorn laughed. "Most likely, some oil rich billionaire will have him in his bed most of the time and when he isn't, he'll be running around the palace stark nude as a pretty decoration to impress his friends. If he lucks out, the old fart will have some sons who will give him a really good fucking from time to time. Most likely, though, he'll have lots of company. Most of those oil men like having a whole bevy of white boys at their beck and call and, when bored, have them put on little entertainments for them, like screwing each other and sucking each other off. Hell, they even have slaves doing that as dinner entertainment, I hear. Of course, we have lots of local customers doing the same things with their slaves. Just part of being a master, maybe," he conjectured. "Tomorrow, with a full stomach and a night's good rest, the new slaves will start their sexual training."

Just as he said that, an obviously exhausted, but extremely attractive 26-year-old Hispanic slave was being led out of a cage by a leash attached to his newly installed collar. He placidly crawled after his trainer on his hands and knees, his shaved butt and banded genitals in full view.

"That boy is on his way to getting something other than a dildo shoved up his ass, probably for the first time in his life. They take a prick up their chute for the first time a lot better if they're totally exhausted and too tired to fight it. It's the next step in a slave learning how to take a good fucking. The initial step is anal stretching and getting used to being penetrated. Most slave training facilities, us included, start this process with a dildo fitted overnight - each night brings a larger dildo being rammed up their hole. In an amazingly short time, a slave gets used to being penetrated in this fashion and accepts being fucked as a slave's lot in life. Of course, most new slaves who were reared where slaves were around know they're going to get fucked as a slave. It's just part of being a slave in this country at least - I suppose most countries. They know it's coming and they might as well accept it now rather than fight it which won't do them a bit of good. The bred slaves we process don't need any of this type of training - they've been stretched and then fucked long before they arrived here and think nothing of it now. It's just a normal part of their life as slaves. That's the way it will be with the newly enslaved when we're through with them.

"Once training is started, slaves are fucked around the clock by trainers and each other until their holes are fully stretched and they are fully acclimated to taking a master's cock whenever requested with no hesitation."

We had entered yet another room devoted to sexual training. At one stall, a white slaveboy had mounted a black slave's rump and was busily humping away up the black's asshole. The black was leaning over a bench so his ass was perfectly positioned for the white's entry with his hands bracing his body in the desired position. As we watched, the white slave pumped a full load up the black's ass and then quickly withdrew and placed himself over the bench with his legs widespread and his body braced for a good fucking. The black, most eager now that he was on the delivery rather than the receiving end, quickly inserted his giant tool up the white's well lubed hole and began pounding the white ass vigorously as the white slave moaned beneath him.

"No prejudice here," Mr. Alcorn smirked. "These new trainees will trade around fucking each other until their holes are fully stretched and practically calloused from overuse. Any ideas about not being fucked as a slave is ancient history by the time they leave this room."

At another stall, a huge black trainer, himself a slave of course, was plowing into a new blond trainee. The fucking was vigorous with long deep thrusts that forced the blond boy's legs wide apart and left him tense and groaning in obvious pain. The stud was pure black, a mountain of muscle, and fully enjoying this opportunity to unload into a fresh white boy. Sweat over his entire body made his body glean in the bright lights as he took the young boy stretched out before him face up.

"You're tearing me in half.... Please, sir.... Please. You're going to ruin me.... Oh. I'm being torn up insides...Please, master... Stop...," the slave whined as the fucking grew even more intense.

"Shut up, boy, of I'll feed you several more inches and you'll really feel it," the black stud counseled as he thrust in even deeper. "Just relax that ass and you'll find you can take even the biggest ones without getting torn up. I learned that real fast when I was first being trained like you."

Taking the threat seriously, the blond boy bit his lip as tears spilled down his cheeks, but he did shut up and just lay there moaning softly as the black prick pounded harder and harder into his fully-stretched hole. Until the black rapist mentioned it, it never occurred to him that the black had probably been exactly like him just a few years ago - flat on his back taking a really big one up his butt and probably felt the same way at that time - like he was being torn in half.

"That's the fourth time that blond boy's been fucked already this morning, each time by that big black stud who is simply inexhaustible, it seems. The black's equipped well for the job of really opening these boys up. When he pulls out, you can see he's over 12" long and a good 6" around. A boy knows he's been fucked when that stud plows him. The blond better get used to it. A North African brothel has already made a deposit of $150,000 just to hold this new slave for later purchase, but, if you'll like the boy for yourself, Mr. Bates, we can easily suggest a replacement for them. It will be O.K. with them, I'm sure, as long as the replacement is young, blond, good-looking, well muscled, and heavy hung. We've got several in stock that fill that bill right now."

"I don't want to interfere in the business until I know what I'm doing, Mr. Alcorn, but I must say that black stud has one of the sexiest bodies I believe I've ever seen."

"He's a keeper, all right, Mr. Bates. We'll make sure he's around whenever you would like him. An excellent choice, if I do say so, Mr. Bates. I fucked that black ass just two days ago as a little diversion and he's as good as he looks - maybe better. He really knows how to work those ass muscles of his to give you maximum pleasure and his mouth is like smooth velvet. Well trained, if I may brag a little. I trained him myself when he first came in."

Turning to the other side of the room, a hugely equipped white slave was being deep throated by a muscular black, equally well hung. A trainer with a whip was lashing the white until he, gagging and choking, had swallowed the entire shaft being shoved down his throat. The trainer made him hold it there until his throat adjusted to the assault and then, with the urging of the whip, the white began sucking for all he was worth using his stretched throat muscles to massage the huge black shaft within him. The black slave was arched over the white's mouth, his pelvis thrust forward as he gasped at the intense pleasure he was receiving. The black's body suddenly stiffened, his pelvis shot even further into the white's face, and the black's entire body shuddered as he unloaded down the white's throat in one huge pulse after another.

"Learning to suck well is as important for a new slave as knowing how to take a good fuck," Mr. Alcorn announced. "No one wants a slave who doesn't have considerable skill in sucking their master off. Before they graduate from here, they can swallow the biggest pricks around clear down their throats without gagging, sucking those pricks so well their owners think they are in heaven, and swallow the biggest loads without spilling a drop."

By then, the black slave was on his knees in front of the white who had just sucked him off and had his mouth wide open for the white slave's gigantic prick to slide down his throat. A minute later, he had fully swallowed the giant instrument and the white was bucking away, literally 'face fucking' the young black slave until eventually he too stiffened, thrust his pelvis forward all the way, and moaned as he discharged a full load down the black's gullet.

Mr. Alcorn drew my attention to yet another black slave on his knees just beginning to swallow the huge prick of a black trainer. "We've taken the collar off this young black for his initial oral training so there's no interference with his throat muscles in learning how to suck a master's dick all the way down. This boy will be muscled out over the next few months as he develops unparalleled sexual skills to increase his marketability despite his just average facial features. Actually, Mr. Bates, he's already sold. We're just finishing up the training before he's delivered to his new owner, a 55-year-old black millionaire, who wants a well muscled black slave that's very well hung. He's going to use him as a 'display slave' on his estate where he'll be paraded around stark nude as well as serving him as a well-trained pleasurable bed partner. According to his new owner, this slave will be kept naked continually, he's going to get loaned out frequently to sexually service his owner's numerous friends and business associates, and he's going to get 'milked' quite a bit in that his new owner likes fresh cream out of a black slave as a major condiment during his meals. It's good to know exactly what an owner wants before the training is completed. That way we can tailor the slave to his new owner's exact specifications. We'll have him fully trained in another two or three months."

"Over here are the fucking benches we find so useful in training the new slaves, Mr. Bates. Ten days after induction, a slave has been fucked over and over on these benches by a variety of slave trainers until the event has become almost routine outside a constantly sore asshole which is now stretched to accommodate even the huge thick shafts of super-sized studs put to them in their training."

Indeed, the room resounded with the moans of numerous slaves bent over the benches having their asses pounded by huge studs intense in instructing the young trainees.

"This slave here," Mr. Alcorn said, pointing to a slave stretched across the leather-covered bench literally gasping as he was rigorously fucked by the 12x5" prick of a slave trainer, "is on his 14th fucking today alone. His hole is sore and swollen from such constant usage but he's learned offering his ass up for a good fucking is the only option given him now or in the future. Consequently, you'll appreciate the fact he's concentrating now on learning how to offer his user full pleasure in fucking him as well as learning to enjoy it himself when it doesn't hurt so bad. That's what his personal trainer is whispering in his ear right now as the stud is fucking him - he's giving him little hints on how to best please his new owner when taken to his bed and telling him to relax so he can enjoy the experience."

"Oh, I haven't shown you the maintenance room yet, Mr. Bates," Mr. Alcorn said, again with obvious pride. "Keeping yourself clean inside and out is an important lesson for any slave."

We entered another large room in which slave after slave was positioned on rubber sheeted mats with their smoothly shaved, nicely shaped butts thrust high up in the air, one slave to each small cell so equipped. Sticking out of the displayed holes were the ends of inserted nozzles attached to small water faucets in the sides of each cell. The slaves, face down, were moaning softly as the warm water filled their guts. Periodically, one slave after another would pull out the enema hose and rush to a communal toilet, a mere hole set in the floor in the middle of the surrounding cages. There he would squat with his legs widespread and empty his bowels with the usual accompanying farts and grunts. As soon as he was finished, he would return to his cell and reinsert the nozzle for another douching of his innards. Only when the water ran crystal clear on expulsion did he head for the showers. Thoroughly scrubbed, he then dried himself off and applied a scented lotion to his entire body until it gleaned. Again returning to his cell, he then lubed his chute carefully with K-Y jelly to ease entry for his forthcoming user.

"Nobody keeps a slave around who fails to keep himself spotlessly clean," Mr. Alcorn opined. "Toward that end, we teach every slave to keep himself pristine at all times, both inside and out, and lubed for action at any time. In fact, the first thing a slave is taught to do when his owner is through using his body is to come down here, clean himself inside and out, and prepare himself for the next usage with a good relubing and application of fresh body lotion. A trainee soon learns a dirty slave isn't worth feeding and, after missing a few meals for being slothful, he decides it's a lot easier to keep himself pristine at all times then suffering hunger pangs. It's an important lesson for a slave to learn, Mr. Bates. Their body is for the enjoyment of their owner and it's a slave's responsibility to keep that body as fresh and appealing as he possibly can if he wants to earn his keep. Same goes for the mandatory exercises that keeps that body in good shape - exercise or go hungry. It's the slave's choice."

"Well, not really," I countered. "You set the parameters of the choice for the slave."

"Of course, Mr. Bates. I can see you have an intuitive grasp of what's involved in slave training, sir. Yes, we set the parameters. Of course we do. That's our responsibility in training them for a contented life in their slavery. It's their responsibility to realize their bodies belong to whoever buys them and they should keep that body as appealing as possible at all times. Otherwise, they're likely to end up in the construction chain gangs or chained to an assembly line bench. We're offering them a cushy position as a Bates-trained slave who understands a discriminating buyer wants a slave's body for the pleasure it can offer him or her, not solely just for its labor potential."

I looked again at the scores of well-muscled bubble-butts sticking up in cell after cell with an enema tube sticking out of it while other slaves were scrubbing, shaving, and applying lotion to their well sculptured bodies, all in an effort to maintain their appeal to an owner. Still others were on exercise machines keeping their muscles in perfect tone. I marveled at how young men, just months ago free, were now deeply engaged in turning themselves into valued bed partners of their potential owners, willing to be fucked or suck at an owner's whim. Then I thought of all those free young men sweating away at football or basketball practices, exposing themselves to agents and alumni in the locker rooms stark nude, and risking lifelong painful injuries every time they played for the amusement of others. Or a free young actor willing to sleep with an agent or producer just to get a two-bit minor part in a movie. What was the difference?

All three scenarios involved trading your body to fed your face - whoring. Of the three, the slaves before me seemed more noble. At least, they could pretend they had no choice in the matter and, as I took in the maintenance room supervisor with his whip in one hand and an electric prod in another, they really didn't have much choice unless they liked intolerable pain, chronic hunger, and the constant threat of being turned into dog food. I wondered what I would do if I had been enslaved for one reason or another (it didn't take much in Pittsburgh these days)? I'll probably have my pretty little butt sticking up in the air with a tube sticking out of it, I mused.

As if reading my mind, a slave nearby, his handsome face ground into the mattress as his gut filled with water for the fourth time, gave me a quick smile as he blushed in embarrassment in being observed like this. I smiled back letting him know I was aware he had no other choice. He softly moaned from his expanding gut with a look of understanding. Again he smiled, acknowledging that somehow I knew where he was at and it was appreciated.

Mr. Alcorn didn't miss much and witnessed the silent exchange. "These boys are coming around right on schedule," he said happily. "Before they know it, they'll be flaunting all they've got on the auction block trying to get a good owner who'll know how to use them properly. It'll be a good home for them and a nice profit for us," he beamed. "A win-win situation if there ever was one."

We entered yet another room filled with numerous small cages, each filled with a manacled naked slave.

"Once training is complete, all our slaves are caged for shipment to the auction barn." Pointing to the nearest cage containing a very attractive boy, Mr. Alcorn elaborated.

"This young white boy whose just turning 21 has been in training for four months as a 'pleasure slave' and knows he will be sexually servicing his owners as long as his looks hold out. After that, he'll probably be resold as an ordinary house servant or perhaps even as a draft slave for heavy labor. So he considers himself lucky to be marketed as a sex slave where he knows his life will be relatively easy as long as he does exactly what he is told at all times with an eager, anticipatory attitude of wanting to please regardless. Isn't that right, boy?" he asked the cage's slave.

"Ah...ah..." the slave made a strong noise while shaking his head in the affirmative.

"Oh, I forgot. This slave was silenced during training."

"Silenced?" I asked.

"Yes. He was responding too slow to our voice-training procedures, so we clipped his vocal chords - that shut him up!" Mr. Alcorn laughed. "We always get a few who just can't learn to keep their mouths shut and no owner likes a gabby slave running off at the mouth. It's simple enough to just cauterize their vocal cords - that solves the problem. Sex slaves don't need to talk anyway."

"I never... well I... I never knew they did that to slaves," I blurted out.

"Common enough," Mr. Alcorn said. "Most animals don't talk anyway and, if anything, it teaches a good lesson. Do as you're told, or by God it will be done to you."

"How many slaves here are.... silenced?" I asked.

"About 10 to 15 percent, I'd wager. But we're thinking of increasing it. We found it brings a premium up on the auction block which just proves my point. Owners don't want a slave with a mouth going all the time. There's better uses for that mouth, especially if they're a sex slave," he laughed.

"Pardon my naiveté again, Mr. Alcorn, but exactly what is 'voice-training'?"

"One of the basic aspects of slave training, Mr. Bates. Learning to speak only if answering a direct question or in acknowledging a command, and, even then, as briefly as possible with your eyes cast downward and in a humble manner indicating total obedience."

"This slave looks almost exactly like a boy we sold to two professional football players, one white and one black, a number of years ago for a pretty heady price. They liked nothing better than sharing a compliant, well trained, handsome slave boy in their bed. The slave was fucked six or seven times every night and sucked off their friends during the day and at parties - lots of use. By 32, his looks and sexual stamina began to fade and his two masters traded him in here on a new young slave who looked just about like this boy we're looking at right now. We resold the trade-in as a house steward/driver to an old Asian man who only used him once or twice a night. But I knew his new job would require a lot more hard work around the clock that he had living with the football players. His 'glory days' as a pampered pleasure slave to two well-built but demanding masters were over. But that's the fate of every slave as their bodies begin to lose their appeal, isn't it?"

The caged slave was mute but not deaf. He looked up at me with total resignation as his prick swelled to full erection and started to drip.

"Don't worry, boy, we'll get you a good master who'll appreciate what you've got to offer," he said as he reached through the cage bars and squeezed the slaves' swollen balls.

The slave looked up with tears in his eyes.

"Look, Mr. Bates, he's overcome with gratitude. Typical of a Bates-trained slave."

In another cage, a slave had drifted off into a deep sleep. He was in full restraint, which meant he had already been 'dressed' for the auction just about to start in the next room. The 23-year-old white male was now collared, tit-ringed, and genitally banded. His wrists were both banded and chained to his collar while his ankles were hobbled together with another set of bracelets connected by a short chain. The septum separating his nostrils was now fitted with a large brass ring which hung down over his upper lip and gave him a totally controlled look. The Bates brands on both his right butt and left pectoral were clearly visible with the scarred skin making a nice contrast with his otherwise smooth, hairless hide. The physique enhancement program had clearly worked on this slave: he was now well muscled, well-defined, and perfectly sculptured. As we studied him, his facial features were outstandingly handsome as were most aspects of his body. His 12x6 prick was semi-erect even as he slept and was well trimmed, his recent circumcision having completely healed, leaving a very nicely shaped organ which was appealing in and of itself. His only defects were smaller than average balls, and a small scar above his left knee from an old football injury.

"How much will a good looking young boy like this bring at auction?" I asked Mr. Alcorn.

We'll soon see," Mr. Alcorn laughed as he led me into the next room featuring plush carpeting, air conditioning, excellent stage lighting and comfortable chairs.

Indeed I did see. The caged white boy was the first up on the block, turning this way and that to best display his body before thrusting his pelvis forward to best display his sexual apparatus and then bending over with wide spread legs and pulling his cheeks apart to best display his closely shaved asshole to the audience. On cue, he pumped his own shaft to a full erection and proceeded until he shot a full load out toward the audience in a wide spray, an act greeted with enthusiastic applause. The auctioneer then had the slave get on his hands and knees and lick up his own cum as the auctioneer slowly twisted a huge 12 x 6 dildo up the boy's hole as the boy grimaced in his acceptance of the intrusion. Once fully inserted, the auctioneer pumped it a few times as the slave gasped while clinching his ass muscles to demonstrate his high level of training. As the dildo was withdrawn, the slaveboy stood up, thrust his pelvis out once again to the audience and smiled broadly. He was obviously extremely well trained.

The audience appreciated this training so clearly evident in the slaveboy's behavior and the starting bid of $550,000 was only a start. His youth and vigor, his high level of training, and the promise of years and years of satisfying service for a master or mistress led to ever higher bids. Finally, the winning bid of $851,000 was made by a couple of old maids in their fifties who planned to each utilize his sexual services three or four times a day. They said they would give him to their brother, a 50-year-old widower when they tired of him where he would serve as housekeeper, cook, yardman, butler, and, of course, his sex slave, since the brother always appreciated a good looking male body. After their brother was bored with him, he could always sell him off to a public brothel or as a draft slave and still probably get a most decent price.

"Well, you've seen the whole operation - from intake to final sale," Mr. Lindsley said after the first sale had been completed. "I have to get back to the office now, but I'm sure Mr. Alcorn will be able to fill you in on any details. If you can come to my office around nine in the morning, I'll take you over to the manor house and show you around. I wouldn't make any decisions this early in the game. Wait until you've seen your great-uncle's own empire before you decide anything. Later in the week, we'll go out to the new Bates' breeding farm."

"Thanks so much for everything you've done already, Mr. Lindsley. I'll be there at nine in the morning sharp. After seeing one of Uncle Randolph's personal slaves at your office, I'm anxious to see the others," I laughed.

"You won't be disappointed, Jonathan. Your great-uncle had a great eye for young slave meat."

"Indeed he did," Mr. Alcorn interjected.

"I assume this little initial tour has been informative," Mr. Lindsley said. "At least it outlines the basic procedures utilized on the newly enslaved who are, of course, desperately in need of the basics expected of all slaves nowadays. Bred slaves have a much deeper appreciation of what is expected of a slave, having never experienced anything else in their lives."

"There's no use spending time here watching the other stock being sold," Mr. Alcorn said. "I'm sure you well acquainted with slave auctions, having grown up in Pittsburgh."

"Well, actually, I'm not too familiar with them as it turns out, but that part of Bates Training can certainly wait for a later time. I'm sure there is more you want to tell me about their actual training."

"Again, you read me like a book, Mr. Bates," Mr. Alcorn said with great respect. He then led me back to yet another room labeled "modeling."

"The new trainees benefit greatly from some good models put before them for study. For that, we use already trained slaves, generally slave trainers themselves now, who demonstrate exactly what is expected of the new slaves once they are placed into duty. Fortunately, we've run across a modeling situation right here," he said as he stopped in front of a small stage with about 20 leashed and collared trainees in attendance.

"That black trainer is getting into position to be fucked and is showing one of the positions most demanded by owners nowadays - being butt fucked from the rear. That black slave shows his tit rings off well, doesn't he, as well as notice how his genitals have been banded to make sure he displays them well at all times. Those rings and bands aren't lost on the new slaves who will be outfitted just like that if they haven't been already. Seeing it already installed on one of their trainers leads to a ready acceptance of the control devices in that if a trainer has them, then surely they must expect them also as a slave - we're trying to get the message across it's just part of being a slave. That black's close body shave isn't lost on the new slaves either. Again, the idea is it's just a normal part of being a slave - shaved, ringed, banded, branded, and collared. All normal for any slave these days - that's the message. That white slave trainer is going to fuck the black good and hard right before their eyes so they can see how well the black slave takes the fucking, thanks the white slave for fucking him as soon as he is finished, and even cleans up the white slave's organ when he is finished. Then we have the black slave fuck the white so they don't think skin color has anything to do with privilege when it comes to a slave. A white's just as fuckable as a black - what makes the difference is the fact they are slaves and slaves are always available sexually for use by their masters. After a few months of this, the new trainees can barely remember any world different than this and just accept it, even seek it out, as part of their being a slave now."

"I didn't know slaves were fucked so much," I ventured.

"That's probably because you said you were never around them much, let alone owned one," Mr. Alcorn laughed.

43

"Believe you me, if you had owned a slave looking anything like any of the meat around this place, you would have fucked them around the clock."

"I suppose you're right," I chuckled. "Here I was just beating my meat several times a day fantasizing about having a slave of my own someday."

"That's what everyone does and when they actually get their hands on some real slave meat, they fuck them every chance they get. That's why your great-uncle trained his stock here to expect nothing less and did a great job of it."

Brett Alcorn then led me to a brown Hispanic slave on his wide-spread knees besides several large cast bronze awards with his hands in back of his neck, his pelvis thrust forward to best display his gigantic full erection, and his muscles tensed for full definition. He had a magnificent body with huge sculpted pecs, a tiny waist, nicely muscled arms and thighs, and six-pac abs. His genitals were tightly banded, placing his organs in full display at all times. His body was completely shaved other than his head hair and his slave collar was fitted out with several special seals denoting the awards he had won. A special tattoo had been placed on his abs denoting his prize-winning status.

"The best training facilities, like Bates, hold frequent competitions to see who can produce the best products for the open market. One such recent contest saw this slave of ours get four different awards: 'Best Conditioned for Sale,' 'Best Trained,' 'Best Prepared for Market,' and "best Hispanic Slave Trainee.' This Brazilian slave is 20 and has only recently been enslaved following his sentencing in Brazil for petty theft. Once imprisoned, the warden sold him to us and we entered him in the contest following his three-month intensive training period here. The last 'boy' we had who won four awards was put up for auction (along with his awards) many years ago and was bought by a young American billionaire whose hobby was collecting awarding winning young male slaves who he could enjoy in his own private harem (and who were frequently shown off and shared by his friends and business associates). The $480,000 he paid for the slave was written off as a business expense which is perfectly legal as long as the slave is used at least part time for business purposes such as entertaining clients. Once with the billionaire, the slave was kept busy entertaining his new master's many business partners around the clock, including more than a few women executives who seem to especially enjoy a well muscled young slaveboy totally under their control. Seven years later, he was completely worn out and had lost his appeal so the billionaire subsequently resold him to a sugar cane farming operation in Louisiana where he was put to hard labor in a chain gang. He died five years later of heat stroke and heart failure but was considered an excellent investment in view of his low resale price.

Studying the awards surrounding the displayed Hispanic boy I marveled at how the competitive spirit had permeated even slave training establishments. It would certainly keep morale up among the trainers themselves and offered a wonderful feeling of accomplishment when one of your products actually won. I stopped momentarily in my reflections to think how quickly I was beginning to think of the slaves around me as 'products' instead of people much like myself. Deep inside, I knew I had to make the full transition to thinking of them as just pieces of meat if I was to be successful in this business. As Mr. Alcorn had said: "Livestock - nothing but livestock." Witnessing how easily even the most recently enslaved could be turned into compliant obedient commodities almost eager to be sold, I was beginning to agree with Mr. Alcorn who was even now urging me to move forward to inspect one of the most provocative slaves I had ever seen - a black, the likes of which I had never even dreamed existed.

"He's been costumed by marketing," Mr. Alcorn said. "What do you think?"

I was so overwhelmed with the slave before us I couldn't even answer, although I thought the skimpy little white rag draped around his torso did add to the overall effect. What really grabbed your attention, though, was him stroking one of biggest organs I had ever seen, even now dripping, with a huge, inviting smile on his strikingly handsome face.

"The market in slaves, especially so-called 'pleasure slaves,' seem to go from one fad to another as fashions change almost yearly," Mr. Alcorn explained. "Black slaves are particularly growing in demand at this time, especially those specifically trained for service in an owner's bedroom. Consequently, black slaves are being churned out at an ever increasing rate at slave breeding farms, bred for outstanding sexual attributes and appealing physical traits. As soon as they reach puberty, they are subjected to mandatory physique enhancement training sessions and very specialized training courses in sexual techniques that guarantee their new owners maximum pleasure in bed. Of course, we're gambling. By the time we're able to market these new products, the demand for sex slaves may take off in different directions - Asians, Polynesians, Celtics, Russians - who knows? But I think a handsome well trained black buck will always bring a fairly decent price, no matter what the current fad is."

"One reason for the current popularity of black slaves is interest in the historical American South where racial slavery was widely practiced and black slaves were frequently utilized for the sexual pleasures of their masters and mistresses," Mr. Alcorn continued. "This black boy here is representative of pleasure slaves being offered in contemporary markets. His sexual attributes, good physique, rugged good looks, and obvious willingness to please are exactly what many wealthy enough to own slaves are looking for, especially those primarily interested in being 'serviced' by a well trained fully compliant slave property. In today's society, many mistresses stock at least one such boy in their boudoirs; masters are equally eager to enjoy the pleasures such boys can offer them. I suppose that's one of the realities of almost any slave holding society, both historic and contemporary. As your great-uncle so aptly put it: 'if slaves are reasonably priced and properly trained, there is always a market for them in somebody's bedroom.' There's a problem, though. Some clandestine puppy mills are beginning to spring up, turning out blacks just as fast as they can be whelped, but they're of dubious quality. I can't imagine where they'll end up, selling for next to nothing. There ought to be a law setting some standards for breeding slaves," Mr. Alcorn shook his head. "Otherwise, Pittsburgh and everywhere else is going to be flooded with genetic defects, runts, the disease-prone, dim wits, and non-trainable rogues that no one will buy at any price. Oh well, buyer beware, as they say, but, mark my words, it's going to hurt the market in the long haul. Some say at least they'll be grist for the factories and construction crews, but, with careful breeding, we can do a lot better than that."

"This slave here," Mr. Alcorn said as he grabbed the slave's penis and gripped it firmly, "we're using for some of our TV ads and promotionals about upcoming auctions. With his collar and other accouterments removed, we're utilizing him to promote what a properly trained pleasure slave can provide for some lucky owner whether they be a mistress or master. Dressed as you see him here by the marketing department, he flaunts his manly attributes and does in fact give prospective buyers some idea of the types of livestock that will be available at the forthcoming venue. We've made considerable money on him already because in between photo takes and TV appearances we're renting him out at $100 an hour or $500 for 12 hours to provide any services demanded of those paying the fee." He began stroking the slave's rampant erection. "Already, he's brought in over $300,000 in rental fees - not bad considering your great-uncle only paid $700,000 for him three years ago and taking into account we can still get $600,000 for him at any slave market in the region if we want to sell him. Human livestock like this have proven to be about the best investment available today if you're savvy to market conditions. It's one of the major reason the price of really handsome and well hung slaves just keep going up and up in today's market despite the huge numbers pouring in from the breeding farms." He let loose of the slave's dripping penis and ordered him to bend over and expose his hole whereupon he inserted two fingers well up the lubricated chute and began vigorously finger fucking the boy. "Despite what we paid for him, this boy brought his first owner a huge profit. You see, Mr. Bates, he was bred on a slave farm not far from where he is located right now and we bought him the moment he was physically mature at the age of 19 so we could get started on his training. But, by then of course, he was already fully acclimated to his status as a mere commodity and knew he was destined to be a sex slave due to the attractiveness of his body. Therefore, he took to his training quite readily."

"I can certainly understand why you use him for posters and the TV ads," I mumbled, wondering how the black boy felt about being masturbated and finger-fucked right in front of a total stranger. The slave wasn't even blushing and seemed relatively unperturbed by such gross violations of his body.

"If you haven't enjoyed a black before, he'd be a good one to bed down when you settle in at the manor house," Mr. Alcorn suggested as he withdrew his fingers whereupon the slave promptly whirled around, sunk to his knees, and began cleaning the fingers with his mouth. "If he suits you, you might consider moving him in over there as one of your personal pleasure slaves. We've got plenty of others around here we can use for the TV promotionals. That way he'd always be handy when you wanted to get a little enjoyment." He paused a bit and then laughed. "I don't know though. Those six boys he had me send over there for his personal use may be ever better looking than this boy - a matter of taste, I suppose."

"This boy sure is attractive," I ventured. "You probably won't be surprised to hear that I've never bedded a black before," I blushed.

"Nothing to be embarrassed about, Mr. Bates. It's really only common among the rich who can afford such things. But, if you're inheriting your great-uncle's estate, you can begin to explore such luxuries now," he laughed as he reached down and cupped the boy's balls. "Yes sir, nothing like bedding a black buck down to let you know you've reached the big time now," he added with another huge laugh and released the slave's balls.

"Well, enough playing around with this boy. I've got so much else to show you in our limited time. I wanted to show you some of our older stock, which sells at a most reasonable price and hence is more affordable for the average person. We've probably spent enough time on millionaire's row," he laughed again as he slapped the black slave's rump in dismissal.

"Older used slaves often offer tremendous value, Mr. Bates. Generally, such slaves have already had three or four previous owners, are now in their late 20s or early 30s, and, if they had been sold as pleasure slaves previously, due to their good looks and sexual attributes, have lots of experience in pleasing their masters or mistresses in bed. That means relatively little further training is necessary in most cases to get them to 'Bates trained' standards. The good side of these older slaves is that they have been carefully selected and trained to start with; the down side is that they are past their youthful peak and beginning to show signs of their heavy usage. Most slaves this old and who have probably experienced considerable use are slower to arouse, beginning to have a little difficulty in keeping an erection as long as their owner would like, and have bodies that are beginning to show the wear and tear of constant sexual arousal. All of this despite the heavy exercise regimes and highly controlled diets they are exposed to each and every day. Most are on continual doses of sexual stimulants by now and, within a decade, even the drugs won't work anymore. Nevertheless, they are still most appealing sexually, are highly skilled in an owner's bed, and offer tremendous value for the dollar compared to their younger and admittedly friskier brethren in the marketplaces."

As we entered another huge warehouse containing hundreds of cages, Mr. Alcorn explained he wanted to show me some examples of what he was talking about.

"Most of these slaves are awaiting auction toward the end of the week where they will sell anywhere from $140,000 to $200,000 due to their advanced age. But with proper maintenance, they can still render their sexual services another 10 or 15 years without too much decline. For those with limited funds, it's the most logical choice. Besides, even when they were completely played out sexually, you can always sell them as draft slaves for at least 50% of what you paid for them."

We stopped by the first cage holding a very handsome brown slave with a magnificent physique and huge semi-erect sexual organs and Mr. Alcorn took a key hanging from his belt and quickly unlocked the cage door and swung it open. Instantly, the contents of the cage wiggled out of the tight confines and, stretching, took a full display position in front of his cage, totally naked, of course, with the exception of his collar, rings, and bands.

"This one was used for years as a personal pleasure slave by a middle aged white executive who had a fetish for handsome mulattos. He's a bred slave and has been trained from birth on for his duties as a sex object and really knows no life outside of catering to an owner's demands, no matter how weird they may be."

The slave smiled beautifully as he spread his legs for a full display of his sexual organs and thrusting his pelvis forward, tensed his muscles to best exhibit his body since his arms were already placed in back of his collar.

"He's originally from an Alabama breeding farm specializing in mixed breeds and who did most of his training long before we was first sold. Since we've had him, we taught him a few tricks about displaying himself properly and handling heavier usage, but he really needed very little instruction. We even thought about keeping him around as a slave trainer due to all his experience - may still do that if he doesn't reach the minimum bid we've set."

"Sounds like a good idea, Mr. Alcorn. What's the minimum bid set at?"

"As I recall, its $180,000 because he's just 25 now despite all the usage he's had. There's at least 15 years left in him yet if you feed and exercise him right with plenty of time to rest up."

"He'd probably enjoy being a trainer for a change," I commented. "That way, he'd be doing the fucking for a change."

"He'd probably like that alright," Mr. Alcorn laughed, "but that's not a slave's choice and he knows it."

"Still, it would be a change of pace for him, unless you think he's getting too old to put it to the trainees properly."

"Well, he's no more over the hill than most of our slave trainers," Mr. Alcorn laughed as we moved on to another cage where, again, he unlocked the cage door and the contents quickly emerged to display himself in front of us.

"This boy's Albanian and is 35-years-old now if you can believe it. He was a former 'cabin boy' on a freighter where I understand he got used around the clock by the whole crew since he was the only slave on board. He was originally bought from an Albanian orphanage when he was 19 and taken to Libya where he was trained and then auctioned off in that white slaves are highly valued in Libya. He's getting to show signs of considerable usage now, I'm afraid, but he's well trained and uses his extensive experience to compensate for his physical shortcomings. He looks more youthful than he is because of his completely shaved body, his naturally smooth skin, and his long shoulder-length hair - all of which makes him still look boyish. Here he is 18 years later in Pittsburgh being sold once again for the pleasure his body can still offer no matter how many seamen from all over the world have pumped his butt over the years. When we bought him, they told us he only got fed once a day because he was generally filled up with the crew's cum in between. Digesting a lot of cum keeps you youthful, you know."

"I always thought that was an old wife's tale," I chuckled.

"It is, but the tale is true," Mr. Alcorn laughed. "This boy is living proof of how a gallon or two of cum a day keeps your body in perpetual youth. That's why there's such a market for 'milk studs' among 40 and 50 year old buyers beginning to worry about their aging bodies. They all swear two or three loads a day from a young stud helps keep the wrinkles away better than anything."

"You would think middle aged women would be drinking gallons of the stuff," I joked.

"It's no joke. That's exactly what they do, if they're rich enough to afford the herd of young slaves necessary to do that. Come around to our next auction and you'll see exactly what I'm talking about. They won't even bid on a 'milk stud' until they see him deliver a big load right out there on the auction block in front of everyone. Some of them even want it in a measuring glass so they can see exactly how much output the stud has as well as feel its consistency and thickness. Those women make no secret of what they're up to and seem to be proud of it," Mr. Alcorn exclaimed with a chuckle. "One of them even told me they use fresh cum as a 'cleansing agent' for their faces before putting on their makeup. What vanity! I always wondered whether they had their slave boy spurt it on their cheeks directly or whether they had him put their output in a little tea saucer for their mistress' usage. Some of those we've sold off as 'milk studs' could tell some real tales I bet."

Moving on to yet another cage, Mr. Alcorn explained the cage held a 28-year-old Italian boy who had most recently done a stint in a Pittsburgh brothel. Once the slave had slithered out of his tight confines, it was obvious he was absolutely striking: dark skinned, magnificently muscled, a hairless body crowned by a full head of thick black hair cut in military fashion, and displaying a huge thick 13" prick already swollen into a partial erection. His well shaped shoulders and pecs flowed down to a thickly muscled abdomen holding in a tight waist line. His butt was muscular, but extremely well rounded and rode high on his body, giving him a true 'bubble butt' that was particularly attractive.

"This slave was kidnapped in his Italian homeland when he was 18 and fully trained by the age of 20 when he was shipped over here for sale to the Pittsburgh brothel I mentioned. He adjusted very well to his new life there and was a great asset to the popular brothel that owned him, having quite a loyal clientele who demanded him by his slave name of "Stud" whenever they patronized the place. There's a lot of Italians here in Pittsburgh, as you probably are aware, Mr. Bates, and they seem to prefer Italian slaves when they can get them. I'm not surprised he was so popular at the brothel even though his looks alone should have sold the goods so to speak."

"How much will this 'Stud' bring when you auction him off?" I asked. "Eleven years of heavy brothel use would wear even a body like that out I would think. From what I've heard, male brothels here in Pittsburgh are very popular and really draw in the tourists as well."

"What do you mean, 'from what I've heard,' Mr. Bates?" Mr. Lindsley let slip you didn't own any slaves until your inheritance and you're still young enough to have needs that must be met. That's obvious from your reactions at just looking at all this available slave meat. You must have visited the public brothels at least two or three times a week. They don't cost much if you limit your time there. There's no need to be embarrassed about using the brothels here in Pittsburgh, Mr. Bates. Everyone does I know of who doesn't own some pleasure slaves himself, and even some that do for variety sake."

"Well, they probably had more money than I did, Mr. Alcorn. I grant you they don't charge much, but I'm afraid it was more than I had if I wanted to eat and pay the rent too."

"But.... But... What did you do, then?" Mr. Alcorn looked amazed.

"Not much," I reddened in embarrassment.

"Oh, Mr. Bates, it's wonderful that your great-uncle has made you wealthy. I'm so happy for you. I can't think of anyone more deserving, suffering all those years of deprivation and hardship."

"Mr. Alcorn, most people here in Pittsburgh don't have any money to buy slaves and a lot of them, like myself, are so poor they can't even rent one now and then for some relief. I think you've spent so much time surrounded by all this beautiful slave flesh you've lost touch with the true reality of Pittsburgh's majority. Most of the people who live here are just downright poor, so poor we often envy slaves who are well fed and don't have to worry about a roof over their head, keeping their jobs, or paying all those endless bills that pile up. Mr. Alcorn, I've even known of some people who were so poor, their creditors forced them to sell themselves into slavery in order to pay their past due bills and, you know what? Most of them didn't fight it much because they thought it was one way to stop being hungry all the time and stop having to live on the streets despised by everyone. Slavery is great for those with some means - they can enjoy all those beautiful bodies in their beds and never have to lift a finger because their slaves do all the work for them, but, for those without any means, it's almost impossible to compete with slave labor. Try to get a job that pays anything at all when it can be done by a slave who works for nothing but keeping the whip off his back and a few handfuls of slave chow every night. And as for our 'needs,' as you so delicately put it, Mr. Alcorn, all we could afford for any relief was our right hand."

"Beautifully said, Mr. Bates," Mr. Alcorn said, properly chastised. "I can see you're going to bring a lot of fresh perspectives to Bates Training that will only make us better at what we do," he said with admiration. "It's going to be exciting working under your leadership. Your refreshing candor, that polite bluntness, remind me so much of your great-uncle - it's almost uncanny!"

The Italian slave looked at me with great respect and widening his legs, thrust his pelvis forward in an open invitation.

"See, even that Dago slave admires your understanding of the marketplace. He's trying to show his admiration the best way he knows how. I'm sure he understands what it's like to not be able to find any relief when you need it - brothel slaves are rarely allowed to unload themselves, you know. Their owners want them hot and ready to go at all times, which means, of course, they can't drain their balls. You and he share a lot, it seems, and he's trying to take care of you in his own way."

"What he really needs is a chance to jack off," I replied bluntly. "And I doubt if you're going to allow him any of that prior to auction - he wouldn't show hard all the time like you'll want and wouldn't shoot a big load when he's told to masturbate there in front of everyone. "

"Well, you're right there, Mr. Bates. Slaves get used to chronic need because they have to - but a poor free man shouldn't have to suffer like that."

"They don't, Mr. Alcorn. They beat off every chance they get," I laughed. "It's the one area they have it all over the slaves. They may be hungry, but they're drained," I laughed again as I moved us on to yet another cage in the huge room.

"What do we have here?" I asked as I reached inside the cage and ran my hand through the slave's thick head hair.

"You'll soon see," Mr. Alcorn said as he unlocked the cage door and the slave inside backed out quickly and assumed a full display position. "

"A 32-year-old Greek man who has been owned by a pornographer who used this slave as the "star" of his best selling S&M epics. He can't meet the heavy demands of the movie producers anymore and he's being 'retired' to the life of a personal sex slave if we can find a buyer for him. We're only asking $114,000 for him due to his heavy usage to date, his advanced age, all those permanent whip scars all over his body, and his rather average penis. The pornographer told me his penis size didn't matter in the movies because he was always being beaten or fucked anyway and no one paid any attention to this prick. But as a pleasure slave, it will sure bring down the value as will all those ugly scars on his back and rump. Still, with all his experience over the years, he could be a real bargain if you don't mind the lacerated hide. The rest of him is really pretty spectacular."

Indeed it was. The Greek slave was 6'4" tall with a heavily muscled body, a beatific face featuring a very nice mouth, the classic Greek straight nose, striking black eyes with heavy black eyebrows, high cheekbones, and a rugged jawline. He wore a heavy iron collar with brass decorations, sported big 3" brass tit rings, and even bigger ear rings. When I took his chin and lifted his face up to study his face, his dark eyes reflected years of excruciating pain and unending agony which he had learned to endure one way or another.

"There's buyers out there who like a slave whose obviously been heavily disciplined," Mr. Alcorn said. "He'll be lucky if he's sold to a master or mistress just looking for a competent bed buck. A lot of boys like this run the risk of being bought by a real sadist - you know, the ones who can only reach orgasm when they're causing extreme pain to their sexual partners. If so, at least these slaves are used to it by now."

The handsome Greek under discussion only shuttered and got a far away look of resignation in his eyes.

"But," Mr. Alcorn added, "a young mistress was in just yesterday asking if we had a very masculine slave available who would be good in her bed but who had been completely broken so she didn't have to worry about using a big buck so intimately. This boy here could be just the ticket for her: his hide shows he's broken all right; his smallish prick would be easy enough to take, even if you were built rather small and delicate as it seemed she might be, and he reeks of masculinity if you ever saw if. Besides that, outside that scarred up hide, he's still damn good looking - something she could be proud to show off, especially if she'd fit him out with a smart looking slave tunic that would cover the ugly parts of him. The more I think about it, I think I'll give her a call and ask her to come look him over carefully and even try him out if she wants to before making a bid. We have a little 'examination room' over at the side there that's fully equipped to test a slave out any way you want - comfortable beds with clean linen, K-Y jelly, an adjoining shower - the whole works for a thorough examination and trial run. We may even be able to get a few thousand more than I had thought."

The Greek quickly reached a full erection upon this last speculation and the look of despair left his eyes.

"What do you think, slave?" I asked. "Should your overseer call the lady?"

"Yes, master. Please call the lady. I'm sure I can please the mistress, master, any way she might want. Especially, master, if I could cover the ugly scars on my backside, master, so it wouldn't offend the mistress. I know how to really pleasure her, master, if you just give me the chance in that little room over there, master."

"Enough, slave" I commanded. "I think your overseer has been convinced to at least call the mistress to see if she might be interested in your body."

When the Greek slave had been ordered back into his cage, Mr. Alcorn led me out of the building into his office for refreshments since both of us were getting a little tired.

"All four slaves I just showed you are being marketed to private owners who are too poor to afford sex slaves in their peak. Most of the buyers will be considerably younger than the slaves they end up buying. Indeed, most of the buyers will be buying their very first slaves - 'starter' slaves as they are known in the trade. For the most part, it will generally be teenagers buying these low-priced slaves charged to their credit cards so they can pay them off over a period of time. Or, if an adult is with them, you can bet they are probably receiving one of these older slaves as a high school graduation gift or as birthday gifts from their indulgent parents who want to start their sons or daughters out in the world with at least one slave to warm their bed and pick up after them. Therefore, these slaves will often have the unique experience of being owned by mistresses or masters almost young enough to be their own children if they had been allowed to have children of their own, which, of course, they weren't unless they had been put to stud somewhere along the line. Slaves sold to these young owners soon discover that teenage masters are very demanding of their new slaves and soon their throats are raw and their ass holes chafed from the constant usage they receive in being fucked six or seven times a day, not counting the times they are loaned out to their teenage owner's friends. The young mistresses are equally demanding, and most pleasure slaves purchased by them have chronically chafed pricks, sore balls, and raw nipples since teenage mistresses seem to be fascinated with a mature males nibs. For these older slaves, at first it seems strange being fucked by a bunch of kids, paraded around stark naked at teenage parties like prize pieces of meat at a state fair, and ordered to fuck other slaves in front of owners young enough to be products of their own loins, but, being well trained slaves, they quickly adjust to the new circumstances of their ownership and perform to their new owners satisfaction without fail. Still, they are in their 30s for the main part and certainly are a lot slower in responding to all the pawing, massaging, patting, and squeezing their teenage owners love to do to their new possessions. But their owners, being first time slave owners, really don't realize how slow they are to respond compared to other younger slaves and never seem to notice their deficiencies in that they are so caught up in the novelty of totally owning another human being for the first time. They would if they had acquired younger slaves to compare them with, but, for that first ownership, the young masters and mistresses are delighted with them. Many of the slaves had been 'gift slaves' anyway and who can complain about something that didn't cost them a penny. Even for those owners buying them on long-term installment plans, the monthly payments are low and it sure beats the alternative: jacking off every night imagining what it would be like to own a slave of your very own. Now, at last, they do, and they aren't disappointed in the slightest - the reality was even better than the fantasy!"

"It's obvious you not only understand the psychology of the slaves you're training, but the psychology of those buying the slaves as well," I said. "I want to make sure you stay with Bates Training - whatever it takes."

"That's a damn thoughtful thing to say. You know, Mr. Bates, you remind me more and more of your great-uncle the more

I'm around you. I liked to work for him and I'm fairly sure I'm going to enjoy working for you as well."

"I've got to meet with Mr. Lindsley early in the morning for a tour of the manor house. It's been a long day for me, Mr. Alcorn, so, if you don't mind I think I'll go home and rest up. Again, thanks for the great tour."

"Mr. Lindsley thought you would rest up a lot better if you had something more than your right hand around," Mr. Alcorn laughed. "There's a company car out front with a driver who we thought you might enjoy overnight. We've dressed him in a old turtle-neck shirt, some loose pants, and even some shoes and a baseball cap so he won't draw much attention to himself back in your old neighborhood - even his slave collar is hidden that way. We assumed your neighbors weren't slaveholders themselves and a good looking naked slave suddenly in their midst would create quite a stir. Dressed this way, your neighbors will just think you brought some old high school buddy back to your apartment. As soon as he's parked the car, take him up to the apartment and he'll strip the minute you close the door. He's well aware of what his duties will be tonight and has cleaned and lubed himself thoroughly. There'll be a leash in his hip pocket in case you want to attach it to his collar when you settle in. In the morning, he'll take you to Mr. Lindsley's office and then will drive himself back here where he can hit the showers and get fed if he's proven satisfactory. Mr. Lindsley's secretary, that fine looking buck his clients like so well, will ask you if your driver was satisfactory and will call us as soon as you give a report. Be honest in your evaluation, Mr. Bates. Discipline is important to a slave's well being in the long haul and anything less than 100% effort must be addressed. We've got a reputation to maintain around here - well," he paused, "your reputation now, Mr. Bates."

"The slave's use is most thoughtful, Mr. Lindsley. I've always wanted to have a nice-looking slave around when I got horny."

"Well, your days of deprivation are over, Mr. Bates," Mr. Alcorn laughed. "You sure one will be enough?"

"Looking at all those beautiful bodies today did get me all charged up, I admit, but I'm sure this driver of yours... well, mine now I suppose... will do for tonight. I wasn't kidding when I said I was really tired no matter how frisky and willing he might be."

"Let us know about that, Mr. Bates. Our training depends on good feedback."

"I'll be brutally honest, Scott. I promise."

Scott Alcorn led me to a nearby side entrance where, sure enough, an institutional looking shiny black Ford Taurus was idling with a beautiful sandy haired, green eyed, well built man in his early twenties stood ramrod straight with his head bowed holding the front passenger door open. He was dressed exactly as Mr. Alcorn had described which hid all clues of his slave identity. Other than his strikingly handsome face, his magnificent physique, and the large very noticeable bulge in his trousers, which even the loose clothing couldn't hide, he looked about like the average resident. A skilled observer of human flesh would notice, however, that he obviously was devoid of underpants and socks, that the pronounced bulge was probably due to a tight fitting genital cinch in addition to being well equipped, and that his complexion was too smooth to be anything but mixed blood.

As I took the driver in, Mr. Alcorn noted, "He's a quadroon we picked up cheap at an Alabama reformatory about two years ago. He's so popular as a 'loaner' we've never put him on the block."

"Slave training seems to have a jargon all its own, Scott," I laughed. "Now back up. Just what is a quadroon, a loaner and the block? You'll have to speak English when you talk to a novice like me."

Mr. Alcorn chuckled as he reached forward and began squeezing the slave's sex organs through the flimsy pants, commenting, "God, this boy is hung." Within seconds, the loose pants tented out obscenely, as the 'boy' gained a full erection. "And hot to trot, it seems," he chuckled again. "But back to your questions, Mr. Bates. "A quadroon has one-fourth black blood; three-fourths white blood or something approximating that. They end up looking a lot like Hispanics half the time, but this boy looks definitely white with a dark creamy complexion. Pretty, isn't it? Customers love them like this, but quadroons are hard to breed - you get a lot of splotchy ones and some that just look sort of muddy. But 50% of the time, you get something looking like this," as he reached forward and jerked the slave's chin up so I could admire his facial complexion. "A loaner is a slave we loan out a lot to some of our best customer and suppliers. Most of the loans are for overnight use, like tonight for example, but sometimes we loan them out for weekends or even a week's vacation of one of our customers. We have about five or six slave boys we keep around as loaners in that Mr. Bates felt it was something we could do to keep our best customers happy at very little cost to us. Frankly, I think he was dead right on that one. Doesn't hurt the slaves any that I can see, and it's just a matter of delaying their sale a year or so usually. Doesn't cost us much, really. And, what was your other question? Oh, yes. Being on the block. That's the term we use for selling off a slave. They're generally displayed on a small block at the auction houses so everyone can see them. That's where that term comes from. It won't take you long to learn the jingo, Mr. Bates. Until then, just ask if we get going too fast for you to figure it out in context."

Mr. Alcorn abruptly stopped squeezing the slave's shaft and looked at the open front passenger door with a broad smile. "He wants you up front where it will be easy for you to have access to his body if you get bored on the drive. This 'boy' knows what the customers want, all right."

"See you soon, I hope," I said as I got into the car as the driver closed the door behind me and ran to the driver's door. "Remember, tomorrow I'll be over at the manor house."

"You'll probably never leave the place, Mr. Bates," Scott Alcorn shouted through the closed window, "once you see the staff your great-uncle stocked the place with."

The driver pulled the Ford crisply away and soon spread his legs far apart as he glanced at me invitingly.

"I'm here for your enjoyment, Master," he said quietly. "Whatever you might like," thrusting his pelvis forward a bit and reaching down to unzip his pants.

"Keep your pants on, boy," I retorted. "We'll be at my apartment soon enough for all that."

"Yes, master," the slave answered, keeping his legs wide spread and open in case I changed my mind.

"You like being out of the reformatory?" I asked, thinking what a stupid question it really was after I had asked it. After all, the boy was now a lifetime slave, not just temporarily incarcerated.

The slave's hesitancy in answering told me no one had ever asked him that before. "Not much different, master, except now I'm sort of a trustee all the time - getting to come and go without being in a cell or shackled all the time. Other than that, it's about the same, master."

"Not really. You're a slave now for the rest of your life, always subject to the will of your master. In the reformatory, you were still a free man - at least when you got out eventually - and you weren't being 'loaned' out for use of your body like you are now," I goaded him.

"Yes, master. But I've found out a slave gets taken care of a lot better because he's worth something and, master, I got fucked steady in the reform school - lots more than since I've been a slave and a lot rougher too, master. Seemed like everyone lined up to fuck this boy from the minute I set foot in that place - guards, wardens, trustees, state officials. Every old redneck in Alabama seemed to get up my hole or down my throat one way or another in that reform school, master. It's much better being a slave, master, especially if you're lucky enough to be a Bates slave."

"What's so great about that?" I asked, fully understanding the slave was totally unaware he was talking to the new owner of Bates Training Center.

"Bates' slaves are so well-trained and expensive, everyone takes very good care of the property and no matter where you go, most freeman and almost all the other slaves have a certain awe of you, knowing how much you cost and how much people would like to own a Bates' trained slave for themselves. Master, I just love being respected like that. I never had that before in my life."

"You know as well as I do that when we get to my little dump of an apartment, I'm going to have you strip naked, snap a leash on your slave collar and then I'm going to fuck the shit out of you over and over until I can't get it up anymore. And I expect you to give me the best fuck I've ever had in my life whether you like being fucked or not. If you don't, you know word will get back to Bates' Training and then you sure as hell will wish you had done a better job in my bed when you had the chance. You call that respect?"

"Yes, master." the slave replied, smiling beautifully. "That's my job, master. You're not raping me. I enjoy being wanted and needed and I know I'm good at what I do. My life has a purpose now it never had before. I've got pride in being a Bates' property and a reputation to maintain."

"Yours or Bates?" I asked.

"Both, master. The slaves of Bates' are Bates, master."

I gave up interrogating the slave after that but knew I certainly wouldn't feel guilty when I enjoyed his body tonight. The concept of slaves' sexual exploitation seemed irrelevant if this slave was any example. In fact, I doubt if he could understand what you were talking about.

When we reached the apartment, it was obvious the slave was startled at how sparse and run down the place was. Most customers of Bates' probably took their loaner slaves to plush hotels, fancy resorts, and opulent homes where the premium goods would fit right in. Once he promptly stripped and his magnificent body was on full display, he did seem totally out of place - high priced quality goods in a crappy setting. He had the little leash carried in his pants pocket already in his hand as he bowed to me so it was easy to leash him with it. That done, I led him to an old couch which I also slept in and motioned for him to lean over the top of it with his legs spread wide so his hole was easily accessible. He understood immediately, and within seconds I had stripped myself and, without any preliminaries, slid up his chute and began pounding away. This was a dream come true. At last I was fucking a beautiful slave boy who seemed totally compliant to anything I wanted and even now was churning his ass muscles to make the experience even better than I imagined it could possibly be. The boy, with his highly trained ass, his nicely scented beautifully muscled body, and yielding the impression he was enjoying being fucked as much as I enjoyed fucking him, took me to heights of ecstasy I never knew existed. No wonder boys like this brought hundreds of thousands when auctioned off. They were worth every single penny of the price and then some. My great-uncle had tapped a market that was limitless. No wonder people referred to him in almost religious tones.

When I finished draining myself into his hole, the gorgeous slave sincerely thanked me for fucking him, the final touch to a perfect experience and then proceeded to completely clean me with his skilled tongue as if he were worshiping my body in some spiritual rite.

"Again, master? Of would you prefer I suck you gently?" the slave suggested, again with great sincerity, as if that would be a great honor if I so allowed. The experience was unparallel to anything I had ever had happen to me in my life up to this point.

"Suck me until I'm hard again, and then I want to fuck you with me lying down on the floor and you lowering your ass down on me. I'm too tired to fuck you myself again, slave."

"Of course, master," the slave answered as he wrapped his lips around my softened prick and strongly sucked it as he ran his lips expertly up and down the shaft while he very gently massaged my balls with one of his hands until it was back into full erection again. Then, facing me, he climbed over my prone form and, taking my swollen prick in one hand to position it, slowly lowered his open hole down over the shaft until it was completely submerged in him. Only then did he begin pumping up and down with his arms braced at each side, smiling at me intently as I played rather roughly with his heavily-ringed tits which quickly became swollen and erect in my hands. As he fucked himself on my prick, he leaned forward so I had better access to his muscular pectorals, the tits attached to them, and so I could study one of the most beautiful faces ever put on a human being.

Within 20 of the finest minutes of my life, I shot again up his ass and was pleased his throbbing prick, one of the largest I had ever seen, was oozing precum steadily as he continued pumping me dry.

"Permission to shoot, master?" the slave asked softly.

"Hold it, slave. Next time maybe. I want to enjoy you a third time if I don't die first."

"Yes, master," the slave gasped as he struggled to keep from shooting off himself, biting his lip and holding his breath until he had regained control of his quivering body.

The third time I had him lay on his back with his legs up over his muscular shoulders so I had complete access to his hole. I pumped him for 40 minutes since I was completely drained when we started. It was, if anything, even better than the second time due to the fact I completely controlled the rate and depth of penetration and hence could keep from cumming over and over again. But finally, I could hold it no longer and shot a surprisingly large third load up the slave's ass. This time, the slave's need was wildly evident with his flushed, sweating body, his heavily dripping prick, and the heavy breathing every animal gets when they are in frantic need.

"May I shoot, master?" the slave gasped.

"Yes, slave," I said. "Well earned."

With that, the slave shot more hot steamy cum all over my face, chest, stomach, neck, and upper arms than I thought any human male could produce, but then, of course, I had never been held in need for almost two hours of constant heavy stimulation.

The slave sensed when he had completely drained me and carefully lifted his body off of my exhausted tool. He thanked me profusely as he began licking the huge gobs of his cum off of my body, starting with my face and proceeding downward until every drop had disappeared down his throat with obvious relish. Then he cleaned my organs off until they sparked and licked himself clean after that.

"More, master?" he asked as if this were possible.

"No slave."

That was the last I remember. After that I fell into one of the deepest sleeps I had ever experienced and never moved until morning where I found the slave curled in a fetal position beside me, the leash still in my hand attached to his slave collar.

"May I service you, master?" was the first I heard from the slave upon arising. When I quickly showered and dressed without answering him, I realized I didn't even know his name nor did I ask it. I would probably never see him again in my life and he would soon, probably that night, be loaned out to some other lucky bastard who wouldn't bother to learn his name either. I motioned for the slave to put his clothes on over his sweat-drenched body which he did instantly. Within minutes he was driving me to Mr. Lindsley's law office where he sincerely thanked me once again for "allowing him to give me pleasure" and I drank in the smell of his body, reeking of my sweat as well as his, my cum still drying on his body, and the smells always lingering after hot, uninhibited sex. By now, he had a rugged five o'clock shadow on his smooth cheeks which only added to his handsomeness. I remembered if I gave a good report on him, he would be fed and then allowed to clean thoroughly for his next assignment.

Well trained didn't quite describe it, I decided as I entered Mr. Lindsley's office. I quickly told Mr. Lindsley's slave secretary, who looked as appealing as ever, that the 'loaner' had worked out well and I had no complaints whatsoever. Somehow, he looked disappointed as he reached to call Mr. Alcorn with the report. Then I realized he seldom got a chance to be around anyone his own age. The favored clients of Mr. Lindsley were all in their 60s and 70s for the main part and couldn't have been too exciting when they bedded him down. He probably viewed me as dream come true compared to the usual clientele. I least I could still get it up on my own! I wasn't adverse to the idea of getting a chance to use him, but in view of the pending visit to the manor house, that would have to wait until another day.

"Mr. Alcorn from Bates Training would like to talk to you, master," the secretary said humbly, showing his training by holding the phone until I indicated I would be willing to do so.

"Yes, Brett," I responded, picking up the phone. "How can I help you?"

"That loaner was just OK?" he asked. "We expect better than that out of Bates' slaves. He's in for some corrective discipline if that's true."

"No," I replied irritably, shooting a glance of disapproval at Mr. Lindsley's slave secretary. "I said he had worked out well and I had no complaints whatsoever as I recall. Not just OK."

"That's quite different, Mr. Bates. Thanks for clearing that up. Mr. Lindsley has got one jealous slave on his hands, it seems, and needs to have his rump blistered good to learn how to report things accurately. I'll suggest not only that, but a good 48 hours without any chow to Mr. Lindsley when I call him later today. Slaves can get downright petty when they're on a long chain. Mr. Lindsley going to have to have to tighten up on that boy of his - telling little lies is the first sign of losing control. He probably thinks because he keeps the old man happy in bed that he's foot loose and fancy free. A good whip and a few days without being fed can clear that up real fast."

"If you have a spare moment, Mr. Alcorn, can I ask a few questions about the business?"

"I'm your employee, Mr. Bates. Have you forgotten? Of course, I always have time for my boss," he replied warmly.

"I was wondering about that slave you loaned me last night. What happens when he checks in with you, assuming you're gotten a good report on him? And how many of these 'loaners' are there, anyway?"

"We have six loaners on hand right now and last night all six of them were on duty and four of them are already back here. But to answer your first question. First off, he shucks his clothes and puts them in the laundry. Next, he douches his hole thoroughly before hitting the showers. All clean again, he reports to the clinic and a slave technician swabs his throat, the lining of his chute, and up his piss slit so we can run a tissue culture for any disease onset while another slave nurse checks him out for any injuries, bruises, or abrasion burns and takes a blood sample. Then it's on all fours and he gets his breakfast chow and a big bowl of water to wash it down. He's mighty hungry by then usually. While we're running the blood and tissue culture tests, he reports to the exercise center where he works out for three hours to make sure he keeps that nice body of his appealing and flexible so he can take up any position or perform anything asked of him physically without any trouble. After that, if the tests are OK, he's caged so he can catch up on his sleep. When we wake him up, it's to the maintenance room to plug himself into the enemas, shower and shave his body again, get his chute lubed and his body oiled, trim his head hair, and get dressed in fresh clothes for the next loan if we have one lined up. Otherwise, he skips putting on the clothes and we assign him some janitorial duties here. Generally, Mr. Bates, they're loaned out at least five nights a week, usually all seven."

"Who to?" I asked.

"Big ticket buyers of the firm, Mr. Bates, who appreciate being remembered that way, some suppliers who offers us some decent discounts, and anyone who's done the firm a favor in public relations or gave us some free advertising," Brett Alcorn replied.

"What if the tests come back negative, or one of them comes back beaten up or overused? It can't possibly always go smoothly."

"I'll answer your last question first, Mr. Bates, because it's the most likely. A few of the recipients of our largesse get carried away with the sudden windfall of a beautiful fresh body at their total disposal and literally fuck them half to death, tearing up their anal tracks, scratching their backs up in passion, tearing their throats with a particularly vicious mouth fucking, squeezing their balls until they're all swollen, or sucking on their tits until they're bleeding. In cases like that, we fix them up at the first aid station and pull them off duty until they're completely healed usually giving them a shot of antibiotics just to play it safe. Sometimes, they're just overused, being up all night trying to please a client without a moment's rest and completely played out by the time they get back to us. Women clients are the worse in this - they can have a boy fuck them until their pricks are bleeding the skin's so chafed or their tits are swollen from being sucked until they're three times their normal size and often bleeding to boot. Some of those gals just don't seem to understand when to stop. God help any slave that gets sold to the likes to them! Nymphos, probably, if the truth were known. Those loaners just crawl back to us, Mr. Bates, and we generally give them at least a week off duty, sometimes even more, to get back in shape and don't loan them out to women clients again for at least a month or so they don't cringe when they first see they're been loaned out to a woman again.

"And the ones that have caught something?" I prompted. "I think it's great the way you test them after each new client. That way you're always sending out clean disease-free stock so the clients are assured."

"Yes, and 999 times out of a thousand they test out clean. After all, we're not just loaning them out to anyone," Mr. Alcorn announced proudly. "Bates' customers and suppliers are fairly health conscious and well educated, you know. I think if they caught something themselves, it would be taken care of right away."

"Probably, Brett, but you never know."

"Exactly, Mr. Bates. That's why we run all those tests which aren't cheap. In that one out of a thousand case where the tests are negative, we pinpoint it right away and generally treat it immediately, quarantining the slave in an isolated special cage until he tests out OK. But we've had two slaves over the years that picked up conditions we couldn't treat effectively. Being good corporate citizens, we snuffed them right away."

"Snuffed them? Speak English, Mr. Alcorn," I pushed.

"Sorry for the jargon again, Mr. Bates," Brett Alcorn laughed. "We terminated them with a lethal prod setting so they wouldn't suffer and, most importantly, wouldn't get loose somehow and hurt our reputation. Some firms sell them off as damaged goods to draft slave contractors and the like where a sexual disease doesn't really matter as long as they are in chains, but we prefer to just terminate them. We're so socially responsible we even cremate their bodies rather than sell their hides to the rendering plants and what's left to the dog food processors like most firms I know of. We have to write off quite a loss that way, but it's the right thing to do if you want your reputation unsullied."

I was too shocked to respond at this latest bit of information and again marveled at my ignorance when it came to the whole slave thing in today's corporate world. "Snuffing" slaves? "Rendering plants for dead slaves?" "Selling their hides when they terminated?" "Dead slaves ground up for dog food?" "Writing the losses off as you calmly electrocuted a slave with your handy prod?" Considering yourself a good corporate citizen for doing all this? Where had I been all these years shivering away in my under-heated little apartment giving little thought to how my more successful free breathen were making and spending the big bucks or how the majority of the population was wondering what setting was on the electric prods waved menacingly over their heads by their overseers at every opportunity. Was it any wonder slaves obeyed even the most obtuse command without question? Was it any wonder slaves gladly opened their holes begging to be fucked? Was it any wonder slaves made sure their masters were totally satisfied with them at all times? And was it any wonder that what I had witnessed at Bates Training yesterday - turning a previously free human being into a slave who was no different than any other animal - was accomplished in just a few months? And was it any wonder that the beautiful young man I had so enjoyed last night could be turned into an out and out whore and be grateful that's all that was asked of him?

"Thanks for all the info, Mr. Alcorn. Again, I realize I have a lot to learn in this business."

"No bother, Mr. Bates. Anytime. I really appreciate the way you're making an effort to get all the facts and find out all you can about your inheritance, Mr. Bates. It bodes well for Bates Training. The more you get into it, the more intriguing it gets. That's why I like the business so well, Mr. Bates, and I'm sure you will too once you grasp the big picture."

"Well, there's a lot more responsibility in the inheritance than I ever imagined, Brett," I replied. "Mr. Lindsley sort of implied all I had to do was settle down in that big manor house of my great-uncle's and let all those 'pleasure slaves' over there take care of me while men like you actually ran Bates Training. You probably don't want to hear this, but I doubt it's going to work out that way, Brett. I'm just not that laid back. If I can't run it, I'm not interested, I'm afraid."

"You sound exactly like your great-uncle, Mr. Bates. It's just uncanny. That's exactly what he told me when he first hired me and one of the big reasons I signed on at Bates Training. I like a boss that loves the business as much as I do. And, from the sounds of it, that's what's happening all over again. Welcome to the family, Mr. Bates," Mr. Alcorn gushed out with so much enthusiasm I could almost see his gleaming face over the phone line. "It's going to be great working for you - I can just tell."

"See you in a day or so, if I don't settle in permanently with all those pleasure slaves as Mr. Lindsley implied," I said in parting, handing the phone back to the handsome slave secretary of Mr. Lindsley who then showed me directly into Mr. Lindsley's office with a fresh cup of coffee in hand.

"I see Pleasure has your coffee ready," Mr. Lindsley said as he gave the slave a few last minute instructions of things to do while he was gone.

"The car's waiting for us out front," Mr. Lindsley said as he walked toward the door. "I heard Mr. Alcorn gave you one of his 'loaners' last night."

"Correction. My 'loaners' if I understood you right yesterday, Mr. Lindsley," I smiled.

"But yes, I had a 'loaner' back in my miserable little apartment and," I felt myself blushing heavily, "it was absolutely the best sex I have ever had in my life... Not that I've really had that much sex to date... but..." I stopped talking while I was ahead.

"Pleasure wants to jump your bones if you're weren't aware," Mr. Lindsley laughed. "You got him all riled up yesterday morning and he's shown a big boner ever since. Even that ancient old crone, Mrs. Forsthye, that swings about ten millions dollars worth of business a year our way, couldn't calm him down last night when I sent him over at her request. She usually drains a boy until he can barely walk home."

The car was waiting with the air conditioner humming as we stepped inside, apparently delivered out front by some unseen valet until I literally tripped over a kneeling slave by my opened door. He was naked save his thick iron collar and the large iron nose ring resting on his upper lip.

"Back to your station, Rasheed," Mr. Lindsley barked as the well built man leaped up and ran back into the basement of the building.

As the big car sped out into the main traffic, Mr. Lindsley said he had arranged for a visit to the new Bates breeding operation the following day. That way, in three days time, I would have gained a full overview of the total operation. At the conclusion of that, he would have all the papers ready for me to sign which would make me C.E.O. of Bates Training Center along with transfer of ownership of all the Bates' holdings. In addition, he had arranged to have the country club memberships my great-uncle maintained transferred over to me along with membership on all the corporate boards my great-uncle was on.

"All your slave properties are owned by Bates Training rather than you personally, so you'll be spared signing all those ownership papers for each slave. That would take a week in itself. Your uncle also owned considerable stock in a variety of companies outside of the slave industry - sort of a cushion in case the bottom fell out of slave markets. I've already transferred all of that over to a new account I set up for your personal use - the dividends alone from those non-slave holdings will give you a good two million a year to spend if you want. Your great-uncle never touched that money - he just let it pile up. You probably will too in that the income from Bates Training alone is five times that in a typical year. It cost him a little to set up the new breeding operations, but, frankly, it barely made a dent out of his operating income. Once the breeding operations start paying off - you understand that's down the line a decade or so - I figure your income will be well over one hundred million a year. If you expand the breeding farm, which I suspect you will when you study it a bit, your income will probably be five or ten times bigger than that. Operating costs at Bates Trainer are going up a little. After all, there's an awful lot of trainers and health maintenance workers over there, but, again, most of them are company-owned slaves and really only cost a little bit of slave chow and a good cage to keep them in since they're all paid for. But costs are going up in that there's more slaves to feed, more cages to buy, and more training equipment as the inventory over there keeps going higher and higher before they're sold off. But, sales are keeping up with the growing number of slaves being trained, so the profits are really shooting up, especially since the price of slaves has climbed recently as demand keeps escalating. There's no danger of overcapitalization, either. Your great-uncle never borrowed a penny. Paid for everything as he went, so you didn't inherit one nickel of debt. You'll never have any banks telling you what you can or can't do! That's very different than your competition, Mr. Bates. Most of the other slave training establishments are running on a shoe string - the new slaves, cheap as they are, are all bought on consignment, the free staff is unpaid except for profit-sharing, the buildings and equipment are all 90% owned by the banks, and the money they get in auctioning off fully trained slaves barely covers what they owe the banks each month in meeting their debt. That's why so many of them go under - six of them in the past year alone. Poor management and undercapitalization are the culprits here. If it keeps up, Bates Training will have a virtual monopoly on the slave training business within the next five years or so. Of course, all that rosy optimism could come crashing down if someone comes up with a more efficient way to train the animals, the bottom falls out of the slave market, or the source of new slaves dries up."

"Well then, I suppose I would just have to live off the dividends of the non-slave holdings," I laughed, and "unable to sell the stock on hand, would just have to spend all my time fucking their handsome little butts."

"Sounds good to me, Jonathan, as long as you remember your old lawyer friends," Mr. Lindsley chuckled.

"Seriously, do you think the competition will come up with some better methods of slave training that could hurt Bates Training?" I asked.

"In my opinion, no, but Mr. Alcorn could answer that better. From what I've seen, the only way you can train slaves faster than Bates Training does is to risk killing them in the process or turning them psychologically squirrelly - literal zombies - so they wouldn't be of any use to anybody. Bates has experimented with some psychoactive drugs, but the side effects weren't worth it. Maybe, in the future, drugs are the answer, but certainly not in the short run. Besides, some of new drugs cost more than the slaves do to start with and with drugs, of course, you have to keep using them as long as you keep the slave. That runs the cost up to more than they're worth in a very short time."

"What about the supply of new stock?" I asked. "Any danger of running out?"

"Not likely. The courts keep coming up with more and more offenses leading to slavery. The new anti-terrorist act alone is jamming the courts with new cases, many of which will end up being sentenced to slavery for life as the simplest solution. Let's admit it, John, slavery does solve a lot of social problems whether we like it or not, and, in our case at least, we do like it. Even if I was wrong there, breeding slaves has really taken ahold lately. Hell, if the courts shut down tomorrow and left the free population completely alone for a change, we could breed all the slaves we need without too much trouble. Look what the South did when Congress forbid the importation of new black slaves in the early 1800s. They started breeding the animals and within twenty years, they had doubled the slave population. By the time of the Civil War, they had quadrupled it - all with out a single slave being imported. Of course, those 'rutting sheds' of theirs were busy around the clock. We can always take a lesson from history. Even now, it's getting hard to find a slave girl in her 20s whose halfway decent looking who isn't kept pregnant all the time. Their owners aren't adverse to turning a little extra profit even now when slaves are relatively plentiful. But, with a shortage, you wouldn't see a slave womb without a puppy in it for a thousand miles on either side of us," he laughed. "People aren't stupid, you know."

"And what about the demand for slaves crashing?"

"Are you kidding? Slaves aren't a fad, you know. Whoever owned a slave who doesn't want more of them? Most owners would rather go hungry than sell off their slaves and the only people I know selling off their stock of slaves are dead men, people who are destitute, or those who are certifiably senile. Take yourself, for example. Before yesterday, you didn't own a single slave. Last night, you had one taking care of your sexual needs - probably for the first time in your life. Are you going to sit there and tell me now you're not now interested in having a slave handy to take care of your sex needs from now on?" he reared back and howled. "Hell, your great-uncle kept six of them around for just that, and he was 61 years old! If the demand for slaves crash, the whole damn economy has tanked in which case the slaves are the best off."

By then, we were parking right in front of a large stately manor house not too far from downtown Pittsburgh. The place was over 100 years old judging from the Victorian architecture but was in excellent shape for an old stone building with a tile roof and leaded glass windows throughout. The front door to the manor was just feet from the sidewalk out front.

Almost instantly after Mr. Lindsley rang the bell, the gigantic mahogany double door was opened by a huge black slave, over 6'5" tall, who was almost startling in his appearance. For one thing, he was stark nude, showing off his extreme musculature and his absolutely hairless highly oiled jet-black hide. For another, he was fully ringed: ears, nose, tits, and the tip of his long penis. Wide copper bands were fitted around his wrists, ankles, upper arms, genitals, and neck. A chain led from the ring in the end of his penis to the door itself, meaning he was locked in place as the doorman, his sole task while so restrained was to simply open and close the door as needed. The picture presented was the epitome of an enslaved male subject to the whims of his master.

"Welcome, masters," the slave said in a deep bass voice as he sank to his knees as we entered, his head bowed appropriately.

Mr. Lindsley ran his hand through the slave's short-cut hair, explaining my great-uncle had the slave chained there except the short times allowed for 'maintenance.' The late Mr. Bates had just liked the idea of having a giant black as a permanent doorman.

"Maintenance?" I asked.

"Oh, time for shitting, getting fed and watered, some exercise to keep up his physique, and sleeping," Mr. Lindsley said. The term is commonly used in describing slaves, Jonathan. If this black boy wasn't at the door, he was in your great-uncle's bed, Jonathan. Your uncle Randolph had a great appreciation for big, well hung blacks." I noticed the black tremored slightly and shifted his eyes at me briefly in a clear sign of embarrassment as his sexual usage was being discussed. It was interesting that even Bates' training couldn't seem to get rid of ALL the old pre-slave responses, although, obviously, all overt responses were long ago extinguished as the huge black knelt there submissively without moving as Mr. Lindsley continued patting the slave's head as if he were a favorite pet dog.

"Then he's one of the six pleasure slaves my uncle kept?"

"No," Mr. Lindsley laughed. "They didn't call him Randy Randolph for nothing. This boy was just part of the regular house staff, almost all of whom were in your great-uncle's bed at least several times a month. The six I was talking about are the six slaves where that is about their only duty, and," he laughed loudly, "believe it or not, they were kept busy more than I or anyone else could possibly imagine. If you take after your uncle that way, and given your tender years, I wonder if six is going to be enough, even given the rest of the household staff being put to greater usage."

"We'll see," I laughed with him. "That black chained to the door does have his attractions," I commented as I reached forward and lifted his head so I could study his handsome face highlighted by the bright copper nose ring welded through his septum. I ran my hand over the smooth high cheeks and then pulled on the nose ring a little to study how it was fastened through the septum. "Any functional purpose for this or is it just decorative?" I asked as I flicked the nose ring with my thumb.

"With a lot of folks, it's just decorative, but with your great-uncle it was functional. He fastened the slave to the door with that nose ring sometimes instead of the penis ring and sometimes used a tit ring for the same purpose. But he told me he often fastened the slave to the headboard of his bed with that ring when he fucked him. Held him absolutely steady, he said, and he liked the look of it - said it reminded him of a horse. The studs are restrained just like that in their stalls when they're milked for artificial insemination purposes; the mares are also restrained like that when they are being bred the old fashioned way."

Again, I noticed the slave's black hide flush a bit to a rich mahogany color while his eyes moistened as this latest use of his body was discussed.

"Come on, Jonathan. There's so much to see in this house that black boy will seem like nothing when we're though."

Mr. Lindsley was right. The house was beautifully furnished in classic antique furniture, priceless paintings, and huge Oriental rugs on marvelously polished cherry floors that took your breath away, collected from all over the world. Walls were upholstered in antique silks and satins, painted with frescos, or featured huge mosaics and tapestries - all with great taste and done by the best-known artisans. The library featured a rare book collection on the history of slavery that Mr. Lindsley said would be valued at well over $1 million if ever put on the market. Many were in Latin and Greek and featured first hand accounts of slave trainers and dealers back in the Ancient period.

"Your great-uncle had each of these manuscripts translated into English which is bound right beside the original papers," Mr. Lindsley said in awe. "There's a lot of wisdom passed down in those translations, your great-uncle always claimed. If we were here with us today, I'm sure he would suggest you study them carefully when you get time. He always claimed slaves had changed very little over the past 5000 years and what worked then generally works just as well today."

"I'm sure he's right, Mr. Lindsley. When I was watching the slaves being trained yesterday over at Bates Training Center and again with that loaner slave last night, I had this strong feeling that if I were enslaved for some reason or another, I would be doing exactly the same as they were."

"Yes, it's a real mistake to think slaves are really very different from us other than the collar around their neck and the brand on their butt. We're all human and humans react in predictable ways. Your great-uncle always said that, although he wisely pointed out that slaves are human animals now, just livestock, but that was essentially the only difference. As animals, they quickly began to think and feel and behave like an animal because that was the only option open to them now. Learning that was a slave's only option was the essence of the Bates' training regime."

"Slaves act like animals because that's the way we treat them," I responded. "That's been true since the very first slave had a collar put around his neck in 5000 B.C. or whenever."

"That's what Mr. Alcorn always claims," Mr. Lindsley laughed. "Treat them like the animals they are, he's always telling me."

Downstairs was impressive with its non-slave objects outside of the fascinating black doorman. But the upper two floors were impressive with its slave objects, the likes of which were seldom seen in any slave markets anywhere in the world. Each slave there was an ode to human perfection. There were whites, blacks, browns, yellows, males, females, short, tall, fiercely muscled to swimmers bodies, blonds, brunettes, red heads, green-eyed, black-eyed, brown-eyed, gray-eyed, hairless, hirsute, banded, unbanded, ringed, unringed, even a eunuch. But all were as naked as the day they were born; all were exceptionally, even breathtakingly beautiful; all were young, sexy, and appealing; and all knew exactly why they were there and felt lucky to be there.

"Give me a permanent marker," I ordered a nearby handsome very muscular brown slave who sported one of the largest sexual organs I had ever seen outside of a horse in full rut.

Instantly it was produced, and, as we went from room to room, all occupied with two or three slaves each, I began putting a mark on their chests as I looked each one over carefully.

"What are you doing, Jonathan?" Mr. Lindsley asked. "Picking out your bed partners for tonight?" he laughed.

"Nope. Uncle Randolph was obviously getting soft in his old age. No one needs all this around - it's cluttering up the place. I'm marking those who I want sold at the next auction. "S" for sell; "K" for keep. Any slave who tries to change the mark will be whipped before sale to where he will wish he was dead and then sold off to the dirtiest, cheapest brothel Pittsburgh has where they will quickly be fucked to death if they don't die from disease first."

The slaves listening to this latest edict shuddered with terror in their eyes and I knew the marks would stay in place. I also knew the word would spread like wildfire.

Mr. Lindsley just chuckled as I went about my task. "Cleaning out the Aegean stables," I heard him comment as he passed the time playing with the body parts of a particularly attractive young 18-year-old male slave with a big "S" I had placed on his chest, and then, with my permission, retired to a bedroom to enjoy a pretty female slave he had found attractive, already sporting an "S" on her breast.

Within 30 minutes, 49 slaves had an "S" mark on their chest, including all the females, those with whip scars all over them, those who still possessed their pubic and body hair, and those not totally masculine in appearance and bearing. The five with a "K" were to my own liking, including the doorman downstairs and the muscular brown slave with the huge phallus that had fetched the marker for me so enthusiastically a few minutes ago. All "K" slaves were 18 to 22 years old, muscular and good looking, were all body shaved or naturally hairless, had rugged, handsome faces, and were well hung without being freakish (although some might argue the young eager brown I had selected bordered on being freakish with his exceptional shaft). All showed an eagerness to be used in whatever capacity I had in mind, whether it was being fucked, scrubbing out the pots and pans, waxing the cherry floors until their knees ached, sucking prick until their throats were sore, cooking and then serving a delicious meal, or doing the laundry. All five were collared, tit ringed, and banded around their genitals, giving each of them a nice protrusion, making their organs easily accessible and fun to handle.

As soon as I had finished, I called Mr. Alcorn directly to send a cage truck and a parcel of slave handlers over to collect the 49 pieces of property for transfer to the holding pens attached to the auction hall with the instruction that I wanted the lot of them prepared for the next scheduled auction. "Be sure to have the handlers bring plenty of prods, whips, and shackles with them - I don't expect these spoiled animals to like this change of circumstances. I want the lot of them shackled for the transfer and a little whip wouldn't hurt either to tell them there's going to be a change in their life."

"I just thought that's what would happen," Mr. Alcorn said back with his usual enthusiasm. "I'm liking you more and more, Mr. Bates. No disrespect, but the old boss had way too much stock over there to do anyone any good. I think he just liked to look at them or something. All of them will bring in top dollar when we get them up on the block - probably close to $55 or $60 million if you picked the ones I think you did. If I may speak bluntly, boss, this needed to be done for a number of years now - too much capital tied up doing nothing but standing around looking pretty. You sure act fast when you see a problem - I really admire that in a man. And, oh, your idea about shackling them and using a little whip is exactly right on, Mr. Bates. Always helps to let a animal know who's in charge, especially when they're facing an uncertain future. Actually helps them in my opinion. The whip sort of removes any alternatives."

"I'm surprised I used the word animals in describing the slaves, Mr. Alcorn, but I was so upset at the waste and their haute attitude that they belonged there by right of their pretty bodies, that's just what they seemed like at the time - a bunch of animals not earning their keep."

"You're learning fast, boss," Mr. Alcorn said admiringly. "They'll know that's exactly what they are when they're auctioned off at the end of the week."

"I'm leaving seven to run the house. It will take that many to keep the place pristine. Five I've already picked out to stay and they will have a big 'K' marked on their front and back. Those to be taken back to Bates Training are all marked with a big 'S'."

"Mr. Bates, you said it would take seven. If you're only keeping five over there, who are the other two?" Mr. Alcorn replied, always quick with the math.

"One is our property having his ass vacuumed out by the police over at Mr. Lindsley's office. Pick him up over there later today, but swing him by your maintenance center before delivering him here. I want him collared, body shaved, and fully ringed before you ship him over here. He's got to look like a slave before he can be over here - just being naked doesn't do it for me."

"You don't go for the 'au natural' look?" Brett Alcorn giggled.

"I can get that looking in the mirror," I countered.

"And the other one, Mr. Bates?"

"The 'loaner' you arranged for me last night, Mr. Alcorn, if you haven't sent him out on a loan already. Have him drive a company car over here dressed just like he was and with another four or five sets of clothes with him. I've got some errands to do and need a good driver. First off, for instance, I need to have him pack up my personal belongings and clothes at the old apartment and get them over here. I'll need to go with him to identify exactly what I want to have him pack, but I admit I plan to take a little break eventually and fuck the hell out of him, so lube him up appropriately."

"I thought you would like him," Mr. Alcorn said, almost gleeful. "He's not out on a loan yet, so he'll be over shortly with our newest company car, all greased up and ready to go."

Finished with my phone call, I turned to the five with a "K" on their chest, all now assembled for my thorough inspection in one of the upper bedrooms. I informed them they would now being working very hard to earn their keep, including pleasuring me and my friends whenever commanded the best they knew how. Any problems and they too would be shipped out for the next auction. I made clear they weren't just pleasure slaves now, but were household staff who would keep the place spotless and in perfect order, even if they had to work 15 or 16 hours a day to get it all done.

"Any problem with that?" I asked.

"No master," was quickly uttered by all as their eyes never left the ground in front of them.

"And, if you haven't figured it out already, I'm your new owner, Mr. Jonathan Bates, great-nephew of your former owner, who, I'm sure you heard, died fucking one of his pleasure boys who will be joining you as soon as the police have finished sucking my uncle's cum out of his ass. But when he returns, he'll be collared, body shaven, and properly ringed like a slave should be - none of this 'au natural' crap. Slaves can't run around like a free man, even if they are naked all the time - nonsense! Takes more than a bare ass to mark a slave for what he is."

"Yes, master," all of them said in unison.

"Well, I see you've got things well organized, Jonathan," Mr. Lindsley said, obviously amused.

With that, the Bates Training cage truck arrived and the numerous handlers soon filled the house, whips in constant motion, as the selected slaves were all quickly shackled and one by one, thrust into the confines of the truck. Yelps and shrieks from the whips biting into their backs and butts filled the air, but otherwise the mood was somber and muted. The five slaves remaining continued standing ramrod straight with their eyes on the ground as their fellow staff was taken to a wholly different destiny in a moment's notice. A new owner now controlled their life.

As the truck rolled away, Mr. Lindsley commented. "A slave has no control over what happens to him. That's why they're little different than any other animal."

The five slaves still standing in position shuddered at the profundity of his observation. The 49 slaves shackled and jostling along in the cage truck were thinking exactly the same thing.

"Get your asses to work," I addressed the five slaves remaining. "By the time I get back I want this place spotless, all those empty cages down in the basement cleaned out, the feed and water dishes scrubbed and sent back to Bates Training, and the entire kennel in the basement scrubbed down and then disinfected with Lysol. Then clean and move your own cages up close to the kitchen door so you're handier at night. Those handlers tracked all over the place and I don't want to see a sign of that on these cherry floors when I get back or your rumps will be so sore you won't be able to sit down for a week. And make sure you're all cleaned out and lubed when I get back. I want you boys ready at all times if you're going to stick around here."

"Yes, master," the slaves chorused back as one, quickly moving down to the basement kennel to start their tasks.

"A nice firm hand, Mr. Bates," Mr. Lindsley observed. "I think I may need a little more of that with that secretary of mine."

"Mr. Alcorn has some advice for you along those lines, Mr. Lindsley," I replied. "He sort of didn't tell the whole truth to Mr. Alcorn this morning when giving him the report on the loaner I had last night. Brett said he was going to suggest a good whipping might be appropriate along with withholding his food a few days if I understood him right, but he was going to call you later this afternoon."

"Well, I'm sure Brett's right. I've been too loose with the bastard lately. He seems to have gotten the notion that as long as he's good in bed he can forget about the rest of it. A good whipping and a few days of short rations does sound appropriate and is generally good for a slave - appropriate discipline reminds them a slave is always dependent on their master's good will and is always a good learning experience."

"I'm sure Brett couldn't agree more," I laughed. "Speaking of short rations, how about lunch? I'm hungry after all that and you probably are too. But I'm going to have to ask you to drive me back here afterwards. By then I should have that company car at my disposal and can spend the afternoon moving my junk over here if it's really mine now."

"It's yours, all right. But, Jonathan, you don't fool me. You just want to get your hands on that slave you fucked last night again. Hell, it's not like you couldn't have any one of those five slaves hanging around here any damn time you wanted, as well as that slave of mine panting every time he sees you. You're suppose to just fuck a slave, Jonathan, not fall in love with them," he laughed, "especially a boy that's probably been fucked by hundreds, if not thousands, of Bates' clients by now."

"Maybe that's what makes him such a sensational fuck, Mr. Lindsley - all that experience," I joked. "Just buy me lunch and I'll overlook your observations about my sex life. You have no idea what it was like living all those years without even one slave around to amuse me. You know, Mr. Lindsley, this whole thing still seems like a dream to me. I have to pinch myself about every five minutes to realize I'm awake."

"Well, you seem to handle it well enough if what I just witnessed right here was any example. You realize, don't you, that after the next auction you will be close to 50 million richer than you are right now, considering that's all premium goods you're selling off."

"Maybe up to 60 million according to Brett Alcorn, Mr. Lindsley," I smiled. "But you don't miss what you've never had."

"I have a feeling I may be talking to Pittsburgh's first billionaire," Mr. Lindsley smiled as we left for lunch. "We'll eat at a good but not terribly fancy place where that outfit you have on won't offend anyone," Mr. Lindsley said rather pointedly. "You're going to have to start dressing the part of one of Pittsburgh's leading citizens," he smiled. "As it is, you could pass for a sassy young slave who's never been collared and owned by a very prudish owner whose had you outfitted at the Salvation Army Thrift Store."

"If you're rich enough, no one cares how you dress. Look at Bill Gates," I countered as we both chortled.

After lunch, Mr. Lindsley reminded me we were to visit the Bates breeding operations in the morning as he drove me back to the manor house. I noted a brand new Ford Taurus was parked curbside with the 'loaner' standing patiently by the passenger door dressed exactly as I had specified. To any passerby, he appeared no different from any free man awaiting a friend to join him. I motioned for him to get the car going while I checked progress inside, where I found all the slaves busily scrubbing cages and stacking newly polished food and water dishes. I nodded in satisfaction and went out to the car where the 'loaner' had opened the curb side back door, apparently fully aware that it was more appropriate for a master to ride in back if his body didn't need to be available for my pleasure as he drove. I made a note of how quickly 'loaner' picked up on things.

"Where to, master?" he asked softly.

"That same crummy little apartment you drove me to yesterday," I answered whereupon the car swiftly moved out into the traffic and was on its way. "I'm going to have you pack up some stuff and bring it back to the manor house we just left, which, incidentally, will be home for both of us from now on if you work out OK."

He slave said nothing, but seemed curious by his facial expression. He was obviously well 'voice-trained' or whatever they called it.

"Do you have a name?" I asked.

"Yes, master. Loaner 3," he replied humbly.

"A good a name as any, I guess, but I doubt I'll be loaning you out much anymore. I may need to change it to something more suitable."

I glanced at the rear view mirror and saw he was surprised and confused at this latest announcement.

"Are you my new owner?" he blurted out, but softly.

"Yes, slave. Jonathan Bates, great-nephew of your previous owner, Mr. Randolph Bates who recently died rather appropriately - fucking one of his pleasure slaves, I understand."

"Master," the slave said humbly. "I thought Mr. Alcorn owned me."

"No," I laughed, "but I could see where you'd think that if no one told you otherwise. Mr. Alcorn is the general manager of Bates Training Center and is an employee of mine. He's certainly boss over all the Bates Training Center slaves, of which you are one of hundreds. No, you belong to me now. You're not loaned to me, I own you lock, stock, and barrel."

"Yes, master," the slave responded with new respectfulness. "I'm your property now."

"Exactly, and I think I'll give you a different name so you remember the event. What was your name before, slave?"

"Loaner 3, master," the slave said humbly.

"No, slave. Before you were a slave - back before you were sold."

"John, master. John Perkins, but that was a long time ago, master. So long ago, I had trouble remembering," he smiled.

"Well, that won't do. That's my name - Jonathan. Can't have a slave around with the master's name, now can we?" I chuckled.

"No master," he answered respectfully.

"I like descriptive names for slaves - related to what they do. That's why Mr. Alcorn's name for you of 'Loaner 3' wasn't bad for what you were doing."

"Yes, master," he replied.

"I'm naming you 'Driver,' boy, since you'll be doing that too now," I announced.

"Yes, master," he said rather proudly. "Always nice to have a good slave name."

"Beats 'Fuck Boy' that first came to mind," I laughed. "You'll be doing more of that than driving me around, I hope, but 'Driver' is more polite in mixed company."

The slave blushed deeply but said, "You can name me anything you want, master. I'm your property now so you can call me anything you want. You can name me 'Fuck Boy' if you want, master. I know I'll be doing a lot of that as you say, master."

"I don't need your permission to give you any name I damn please, slave, so you better shut up while you're ahead. It's 'Driver,' at least for now, slave."

"Yes, master," the slave responded, somewhat flustered that he had upset me somehow.

Shortly after that exchange, Driver and I were inside the apartment and I pointed out the clothes, notebook computer, my CDs and DVDs, and a few other belongings I wanted moved to the manor house as he was shucking out of his clothes as if by habit. I didn't stop him and once again admired the body on this magnificent possession I had now inherited.

"That's good, Driver. Whenever we're inside, I want to see you butt naked at all times like most slaves, but when we're outside and you're driving me around, I want you dressed just like you are today. That goes for your new home as well as just here. They're scrubbing out a cage for you over at the manor house right now in that you'll be staying in the kennel there from now on so you're always handy. No more loaning you out to strangers every night. But you're going to get fucked just about as much - it's just that your new master is going to be the one fucking you from now on for the main part."

"Yes, master," the slave said, obviously pleased at what I was saying. Then I thought, if I were in his place, I would probably be quite pleased too. The new arrangement beat being loaned out every night to perfect strangers to be fucked until you could barely stand up and then be tested rather crudely the next morning to see if you had picked up some disease or other. It was like being promoted from a whore on consignment to a courtesan. "Would you like to fuck me before I start packing, master?"

"Yes," I responded, noting he had a full erection as soon as he had the last of his clothes off. "Over the couch, boy," I motioned, "with your legs wide apart for the first time around."

"Yes, master" was the last thing he said outside of a few grunts and groans as I took my pleasure with him both all the way up his hole and later clear down his throat until his neck muscles were milking my shaft. It was just as transforming an experience as last night had been and, 40 minutes later, I was soaked in sweat, completely drained after three orgasms in succession, and felt like I was floating. It had been even better than before, I reflected, if that was possible as I felt him cleaning my flaccid shaft with his mouth now that I informed him I was through using him for the afternoon. His prick was still rampant since I hadn't let him shoot with all my usage. I wanted him ready to go for an evening bout and he seemed to know that already - at least he never asked permission to cum this time around. Without prompting, he got up off his knees and began the packing tasks while I watched his sweaty body working away in all its glory as I fell into a long nap. When I woke up, everything had been packed and, dressed, he had transported it all to the car so as to not offend any of my neighbors with his nakedness. Driver was kneeling beside the old couch, naked once again, obviously expecting to be fucked again before we left. Why not, I thought, and this time I had him fuck himself on my pole as I just lay on the couch enjoying it with no effort on my part other than playing with his big tits so nicely ringed just for that purpose.

"Mother of God," I yelled as I shot another huge load up his ass. "I don't know how much of this I can take," I said aloud as if it were the slave's fault.

"Sorry, master," Driver said submissively. "Did I pump too fast or hard, master?"

"No, Driver, nothing to do with you. You serviced me just fine. It's just that it's been a long afternoon for me. I'm not used to being drained this much within a few hours."

The slave said nothing, but I could tell studying his face he thought my response was novel, to say the least. I figured when he was loaned out to a women, or even some men probably, he had been drained considerably more than that in a four hour stretch.

I quickly dressed, motioning for him to do the same, and he drove us back to the manor house where he was oriented by the other slaves as to the whereabouts of his new cage, the location of the slave's 'maintenance' station with its store of enema equipment, body lotions, lubes, shaving supplies, first-aid products, and dirty clothes hamper. He was given a small space in the front closet to store his clothes for when he was serving as my driver before joining them in performing the many chores I had assigned for a general clean-up. He reeked of sex sweat from his recent activities - a scent instantly recognizable to the other slaves.

I overheard the super-hung brown slave asking him as they headed for the kennel in the basement, "the master just fuck you?"

"Yes," he replied without a trace of embarrassment.

"Thought so," the other slave replied. "Could smell it the minute you came in the house. You're just like me, slave. Stink to high heaven when you've been fucked good and proper. I thought only us colored boys broke out with that sex sweat when we're fucked, but I found out soon as I was a slave's skin color has nothing to do with it. Some do and some don't. You learn a lot when you're a slave."

"You're right about that, slave," Driver answered without a trace of bitterness or regret in his voice.

After that, both were so busy all talking ceased, but I was looking forward to fucking the brown slave when I felt up to it to see if he was right about breaking out in a full sex sweat when I fucked him.

That night, I ate at a fast food joint using the company car and then went to a movie. I needed a break from gorgeous slaves everywhere I looked, fancy manor houses, fucking beautiful totally compliant bodies, and worrying about the responsibilities of running a literal empire based on the sale and training of human flesh. The movie was a light comedy and just the ticket for some real relaxation. When I returned, I quickly found my bed and went to sleep, ordering all the six slaves to their cages despite them begging with their eyes for some usage so they could get off. Slaves were often in great need, I knew, but, hell, so was I for years and years. Besides, Mr. Alcorn claimed keeping slaves in constant need was important in their discipline.

The next morning, the house slaves were already busy cleaning and fixing me a decent hot breakfast which was served bedside. The server, the brown slave with the huge tool, stood right beside the tray, his erect prick wavering in the air as I began eating.

"Some cream, master?" the brown slave asked, pointing politely to his huge swollen shaft and then to my coffee cup as well as a warm muffin.

I didn't know what he meant since I didn't see any cream pitcher on the tray.

The slave sensed my confusion and clarified himself. "My cream, master, fresh and tasty. Old master Bates had lots of fresh cream every morning. Had three of his slave boys up here every morning emptying their balls. Claimed it kept him youthful - lots of mistresses and masters have a nice drink of stud cream now, master. I can get some others up here too if you find I don't produce enough for you, master."

"No cream, slave. Not now, at least. You just keep it in your balls for now. Skedaddle, I don't like slaves around when I'm eating."

"Yes, master," the slave said, obviously disappointed he wasn't going to get drained that morning. But he did promptly leave the room after a quick bow of obedience, his giant prick waving in front of him.

After eating the breakfast, sans the 'cream,' I quickly showered, shaved, and threw some clothes on. Then I took the Ford and headed for Mr. Lindsley's office since I didn't want Driver hanging around all day when he could be put to useful work at the manor house. Besides, I didn't particularly want one of the house slaves observing first hand a breeding operation until I understood it myself better.

When I arrived at the Lindsley law firm, Pleasure, the secretary, was obviously in pain as he sat down and, from the way he studied the breakfast roll in my hand, very hungry. Mr. Lindsley had obviously addressed the problem of a "slave on too long a chain" as Mr. Alcorn described it. That slave was on a short chain now, judging from the look in his eye which was totally submissive, begging for forgiveness.

Mr. Lindsley insisted on driving since he knew exactly where we were headed and, after discussing the disciplining of his slave Pleasure and his nosy inquiry into how I liked the 'loaner' slave a second time around, assuming, of course, I had fucked him again yesterday afternoon as soon as he and I had parted, we arrived at a rather run down old farm featuring a number of barns and outbuildings.

"I named the 'loaner' you were inquiring about 'Driver' to denote his major activity from now on. I've decided to use him as a chauffeur primarily," I informed Mr. Lindsley as we walked into the farm's entrance.

"Save it, Jonathan. You might fool the public with that new name, but not an old goat like me. You should have named him 'Fuck Boy' if you were halfway truthful. How many times did you plug that slave after you left me, anyway?" he laughed.

"Well, I did consider naming him just that, but thought it was more polite to name him 'Driver' for your information, Mr. Lindsley. And, as to your second question, four. And I'm still completely drained from the experience," I smiled back.

"If that slave hadn't had so much use, he wouldn't have been able to walk after that," Mr. Lindsley observed. "How about trading him for Pleasure some afternoon? Give me a chance to try the new wonder boy out and give you a chance to make Pleasure's day now that he's been properly humbled as to his proper station in life."

With that, we entered the first building where the primary desk was labeled "Studmaster."

"Hans, I want to introduce you to your new boss. Mr. Bates, this is Hans Schreiber, the man that makes this place hum."

Hans Schreiber, a portly but middle-aged man looking to be of strong German descent, promptly stepped forward to shake my hand strongly, mumbling something in his thick accent about how he was glad I was taking over the firm and how grateful he was I was visiting this new operation so early in my tenure.

"Well, I like to see what's going on in all aspects of the business," I responded, "and, of course, we're always interested in a steady supply of the highest quality slaves down the line. That is, if they can be produced predictably, on schedule, at the lowest possible cost, and are better than anything now available."

"Wow! You sure don't waste any time letting people know your expectations, Mr. Bates. I feel like I'm on the spot after all that."

"You are, Mr. Schreiber," I replied simply. "That's exactly where you're at."

"Let's start with your background, Mr. Schreiber. What qualifications do you have for breeding slaves?"

"Er, uh... I was a horse breeder for 18 years back in Germany, Mr. Bates, practically my whole adult life," he started out, obviously caught off guard having to explain his qualifications. "The farm I was at specialized in breeding some of the best draft horses in the whole country, including the famous Bavaria breed, noted for its strength and total non-variability from one horse to another. We were working on a new breed of white riding horse to be called "White Wonders" when I quit to take this job here and we were having quite a bit of success. I think within another year or two, you'll start to see some of those White Wonders on the market - they're bred for durability, smarts, and riding comfort. As for breeding slaves, Mr. Bates, I can't see where it's any different than breeding horses, at least so far. Seems a little easier, actually, in that you can work steady, there being no necessity for females to be putting out the proper scent to get the males interested like with horses. That's about it for qualifications, I guess."

"Sounds good," I said. "What are your working on now? Some new breeds or just getting the quality up as high as you can, Mr. Schreiber?"

"Both, actually, Mr. Bates," warming up to his brash new boss who seemed to show considerable interest in what he was doing. "First off, we're trying to get the best quality we can out of what we've got to work with - and we've got some mighty find breeding stock on hand if I do say so myself. And, yes, Mr. Bates, we've started working on two specialized breeds of slaves: 'Black Boys' which we hope to be a large, sturdy male work slave that is disease resistant, long lived, and practically indestructible in intensive labor situations but not much on looks and a much more expensive type of slave we're tentatively calling 'Bates' Best' which we hope are the best looking, sexiest, easiest to arouse, and inexhaustible slaves to ever hit the pleasure market in both male and female versions."

"Clear-cut goals - that's good. I'm especially interested in your long-term projects of actually developing specialized slave breeds. Long overdue in this genetically sophisticated age, if you ask me. There's no reason this can't be done in relatively short order, Mr. Schrieber. Look at what they've done with dogs and horses. I understand that was accomplished in less than eight generations. If we cheat a little by starting with the most highly selected stock to start with, that might be cut down to five generations at most - with slave stock we're talking about, let's see, about 18or 19 x 5, that's just 90 to 95 years away. We won't see it, but out grandchildren will. In the interim, we can get fairly close: breeding hundreds of broods from a given stud will help - they're all half-brothers but that makes the genes a lot more similar. And the down side of incest has been vastly overstated, I glean from the research. My understanding is you don't run into any problems 90% of the time - especially with breeding brothers to sisters and mothers to their male offspring. Taking the risk of a few defects we can throw away from time to time, I'm of the opinion we can have a new exclusive slave strain on the market within half the time you'll normally think - well within our live times, Mr. Schreiber - a mere 45 to 48 years if everything went well and you were willing to sterilize the majority who you didn't want contaminating the gene pool."

"Mr. Bates," Hans Scrieber said excitedly as he practically hugged his new boss, "you're a studmaster's dream come true. You really knows the ends and outs of breeding. You'll be the first person I ever worked for that really understood the whole process of developing a new breed and all the problems associated with it. We even share the same goal, Mr. Bates. We both want some new clearly distinctive slave breeds out there in the marketplace during our lifetime."

"Exactly, Mr. Scrieber," I replied. "Now let's see the stock you've got on hand."

As we walked toward the first outbuilding, Mr. Lindsley commented that cleaning out the Aegean stables yesterday was nothing compared to that little display of mine which only a German could appreciate. "Me? I like the excitement of finding the exception myself out in the marketplaces. The way you two carry on, you could order them out of a catalog and have them delivered the next day, exactly as pictured."

"That's where the market's headed," I replied. "But you'll be happy to know they still produce the stock the old fashioned way - one fuck at a time. But even that may give way to artificial insemination once the breeds are firmly defined."

"That's when all the fun ends," Mr. Lindsley commented dryly. "At least for the slaves."

"I think you'll find the stock here doesn't necessarily view their duties as all fun," Mr. Schrieber added. "You'd be surprised how many studs don't like fucking all the time, once they're actually in a breeding operation. For the most part, all that bragging in the holding pens of any marketplace about how they hope a buyer will pick them to stud the rest of their lives and then they'd be in slave heaven is just bravado. Put to the test of an actual breeding operation, they quickly get tired of it and have to be held under firm discipline to perform when scheduled."

"And the women slaves?" Mr. Lindsley asked. "They're always wanting to be loved - well, here's their chance."

"Even the most naive slave girl soon learns being fucked and being loved are two entirely different things. A slave is fucked; a free woman might, if she were lucky, be loved somewhere along the line. And being pregnant all the time isn't much fun either, even though they do seem to get used to it soon enough. We do try to make their lives as comfortable as possible if they cooperate completely with our goals, even throwing them a good looking stud just for the fun of it sometimes as a special reward.

"For both the male and female slaves, though, Mr. Lindsley, nothing makes them feel more like an animal than when they know they're being bred exactly as any other animal. But they think better than other animals, of course, so they're fully aware they're making new slaves just like them that will be bred just like them and there is no chance of ever breaking the cycle. That's why they get a little hard to manage sometimes, in my opinion. Inappropriate for a slave, I know, but it's there nevertheless. You have to let them know right up front that's just part of their life and they have to deal with it without letting it interfere with their owners' plans for their body. Nothing complicated about it, but it's got to be digested one way or another."

We had entered a series of stalls where, as we spoke, stud slaves were being put to females strapped down on 'rutting benches' positioned at just the right height for full and easy penetration. It was easy to see why the studs had been chosen for this task: to a man they were well built, extremely handsome, and very well hung - exactly what brought top prices at any marketplace for male slaves. The female stock beneath them were perfect counterpoints: beautiful, physically sturdy, and obviously built for reproduction with wide hips, large vaginas, and good sexual response. As the couples rutted away to the accompanying groans, sighs, grunts, and gasps, sweat quickly covered the stud's sleek bodies and, soon enough, each one arched his back as his body tensed and another load was deposited deep within the woman. As soon as the stud stopped pumping, a slave supervisor, whip in hand, felt the spent stud's balls to make sure he had emptied completely. Only then, with a slap on the rump, was the stud allowed to withdraw whereupon he was promptly washed, dried, and powdered, had a leash fastened to his collar and was led back to his familiar cage located apparently in an adjoining room.

This time, however, I told Hans Schrieber to have the studs brought over for my personal inspection. The first one finished was promptly before me, his hairless heavily muscled body glistening in sweat, still panting a bit, and still, surprisingly, semi-erect. As he stood before me in full display position upon order of his attendant, I checked out his muscles, turned his face one side and then the other to study his features, and then stroked his large shaft, still very hot to my touch and still throbbing from his recent orgasm.

"How many times a day is this one bred?" I asked Mr. Schrieber.

"Three times, seven days a week," he replied, "until his sperm count goes down or he has trouble getting it up properly. They last about five years that way if we start them young enough. After that, we sell them off - there's quite a market for phased out studs surprisingly."

Turning to the slave I was stroking, I asked, "And you, slave, are you performing your duties the best you can?"

"Yes, master," the slave replied, still panting a little from his recent efforts.

"It's quite a privilege to get to fuck all these beautiful women day in and day out, isn't it, slave?" I probed.

"Yes, master, but…. "

"Yes, slave. Speak out!"

"Master, that's all I do, just fuck when they tell me to, exercise, eat and sleep. My balls are always sore and I…."

"Go on, slave. You have my permission to speak."

"I wish I could do something else occasionally, master. I never thought I would say this, but even a slave can get tired just making babies all the time. I'm sorry, master… I shouldn't have been so forward…. I apologize, master," looking at the whip in the attendant's hand getting unfurled.

"Its OK, slave. I ordered you to speak out and you did. Telling the truth to his master never hurts a slave in the long run."

"No master," the slave looked down at the ground, unconvinced, as I continued to stroke him to see if he could obtain a full erection this quickly after emptying his balls.

"Mr. Bates owns you now, slave, so you're lucky to speak directly to your owner this way. I'm sure you want to thank him for listening to a mere slave," he prompted.

"Thank you, master," the slave promptly responded both verbally and with a full erection.

By that time, another slave had emptied himself and had his organ cleaned off before being led over to me. This slave was a light brown with impressive musculature, striking good looks, and exceptionally large sexual organs.

"You enjoying your life on stud, slave," I asked.

The slave shook his head in the affirmative, but did not respond verbally.

"He's been silenced for some reason or another. Long before we got him," Mr. Schrieber replied, "but we've had no trouble with him doing exactly what we expect him to. He's been at this for about six years, I understand, long before I got here."

I studied the slave carefully, noting his large protrusive nipples, thick muscular neck, well rounded shapely butt just begging to be fucked itself, and his facial features that were so fine he looked almost feminine were it not for all those muscles everywhere and the huge organ between his legs. He reminded me... of... Who was it? Oh, yes. It hit me. The brown slave back at the manor house that was hovering over my breakfast tray offering me some of his cream.

"I've got a slave I think I'll send out here for a while that might be good at this," I commented as I began kneading the big balls of the brown slave in front of me, now feeling a little empty as he stood there placidly.

"That's great, Mr. Bates. This slave is about played out, I'm afraid. He's into his sixth year on the rutting benches and he's beginning to get a little slow on the uptake, if you know what I mean. It's about time we put him back on the auction block. He'll still bring us a good $400,000 or so - middle aged divorcees are crazy about these boys because they can use them all night long if they want and still get them relatively cheap."

"Well, keep him at it until I send his replacement out. I really haven't tested the new boy out thoroughly. My great-uncle used him, apparently, as a milk stud for his dietary supplements. In fact, I'm told, at 61 he was swilling down the full output of three young studs a day in his quest to stay young. The one I'm thinking of might be close to being milked dry by now, he may not be any good at anything but jerking off at this point, or, for all I know, he doesn't even know how to fuck properly, although I doubt it. I do know he's sure as hell hung for the job - makes this boy look puny by comparison and I do know he's about as good looking and well built as a slave boy gets at this stage in the breed's development. I'll run him through the hoops over the next week or so, and if he's as good as he looks, I'll send him out and you can retire this boy here to the marketplace. This boy should bring even more at a good auction with all those divorcees and widows since he's silenced. That way, he can't tell any secrets or spread gossip about his new mistress. But for myself, I'm not into stud's milk - at least not yet. Maybe when I get wrinkled and feeling old, I'll change my mind."

Hans Schrieber laughed heartily. "That fad was just catching on in Germany when I left, Mr. Bates. Every old man I know was looking for a fresh young stud for that very purpose. Driving the prices way up."

The next stud had finished his chore and was ready for my inspection, his sweating body looking totally controlled with the collar around his neck attached to the short leash held by his attendant.

"You're lucky, slave. Some other breeding places are switching over to artificial insemination. Then you're just chained down and sucked dry by a machine twice a day and that's it. Some places you never see the light of day until years later when your sperm counts goes down. Here you get to do real fucking and all the pleasure that involves. I know many a slave all over the city that's never allowed to dump a load no matter how hot and bothered they get - their master's consider it a form of good slave discipline. They're kept in a chronic state of sexual need - barely know what's it like not to have a big hard-on between their legs and constantly feeling pressure in their big swollen balls. You're one lucky slave getting to serve stud out here at this breeding shed."

"Yes, master, I know, master. My last owner was just like you describe, master. I never got to shoot off because he wanted me showing hard all the time. Liked the look of a slave in chronic need, he said. Claimed it was the best form of keeping slaves totally obedient. I don't know about that, master, but I do know I felt so needy I would shoot off at least every day or so just when someone touched by body I was so horny all the time, master. Every time that happens, I got beaten again half to death so I really tried, master, but I just couldn't sometimes."

He began to cry at the remembrance. "Most slave boys kept in that constant need like you say, master. That's why I'm so grateful and appreciative of being out here doing what men are supposed to do, master, even if I am just a slave."

"That's quite a little speech, slave, but that's not up to you, as you well know. Those are all a master's decision, just like fucking on command here is your master's decision. It's just that you like that decision more than some others you have experienced as a slave. But, remember, a slave's duty is to obey, not sitting around judging what happens to them. That's mighty dangerous for a slave, boy."

"Yes, master," the slave said as his eyes shot down in shame. "My mouth is working faster than my brain, master."

"Precisely, slave. That's why many slaves are being silenced these days," I warned. With that, I checked out his body and found it flawless. He was, I judged, an excellent choice if genes were to be passed on to another generation. As a bonus, he obviously wasn't dim-witted, either.

"I'm impressed, Mr. Schrieber," I announced. "I really don't have time to look over all the breeding stock if I'm going to see some of your research projects."

"I was hoping you would ask, Mr. Bates," Hans Schrieber replied with even greater enthusiasm. "I hope you're impressed."

We left for another building a good block away from the rutting stations and the adjoining holding cells.

"This is our 'Black Boys' secret project, Mr. Bates. I've already told you what we're after as a market product. I want to show you how far along we are at this point with just three yearly crops produced so far. We're taking every short cut I know of and then some to speed it up.

"First, we're using one prototype stud: the best we could possibly fine in a worldwide search." Turning to a nearby cell, he pointed to a huge hairless black that looked like a cross between a handsome human strong man and a hairless gorilla. His musculature looked like he had been on heavy steroids since birth, his face was passive with an obedient look to it despite the fierceness of his body, and his sex organs were elephantine - more animal than human. "All paternal genes are from this one source for the new breed."

"Second, all brood stock are related - either sisters or first cousins so we can reduce gene variability down as much as we can. They are kept in the holding tank over there," pointing to a huge cage containing a good 20 women, all totally jet black, all very large and muscular, all big boned and wide in pelvis for good child bearing, and all strong as oxen. As you can see, they all look amazingly alike - practically like twins. It took eight months just to buy up stock with the relationships and blood lines we were seeking. Like the stud, they were found in African markets. As you would expect, they are all pregnant again currently, but their first two batches of offspring are what's interesting. For that, Mr. Bates, we need to step into the next room - the nursery as we call it, where we keep the offspring once they are born to be wet nursed and trained by a specially trained troupe of castrated slave men and sterilized women so there is no danger of bad genes getting into the picture."

We stepped into the next room, and I was astounded. There were over 40 big, black babies of both sexes crawling around the floor, huge for one and two year olds, and hyper-developed for their age, but all looking almost exactly alike other than the sex differences. They were exactly the same shade of skin color, had the same body structure, same facial features, and the same height to weight ratio - even at that infantile level. Female 'puppies,' as they were called, were kept in one cage; male 'puppies' in another so the similarities were all the more startling.

"The test we use is can you tell them apart by any means? Faces, fingers, sex organs, rumps, skulls? If so, they're shipped out to another regular slave nursery to be raised for the orthodox market. If not, they're kept here until any significant differences emerge. Our hope is that when they are of an age where we can breed them, we'll have at least 5 of 6 of each sex out of each year's crop that will form the genesis of our new 'Black Boy' breed. At that point, we're going to pick a single prototype stud again and start all over until, we hope, within 19 years to have a marketable breed, everyone of which will look exactly alike, and, even better, act exactly alike. They'll be ugly, I grant you, but the world will have never seen a slave better equipped for the labor market. Nor will they be able to get better value for their money. These slaves should last through anything a corporation or municipality or any private owner can put them through. They should be stronger than anything out there on the market, more compliant to even the harshest demands, adaptable to even the worst environmental conditions, and so disease-resistant they could live through a plague. Our studies show so far all that's true even now in the two-year-olds comparatively, but they do take a lot more food to feed all those muscles, and it takes a firm hand to get maximum work out of them. Most of them will end up in chain gangs under a whip anyway, so that part really doesn't matter too much probably. We figure the increased food costs are offset by their survivability and lack of need for any medical services along the way. They have immune systems borrowed from the animal world, it seems."

"I see you have them collared already, Mr. Schrieber," I noted.

"Yes, we plan to always have a collar on them so they can't remember not wearing one. It marks them even now as what they are - livestock," Hans replied.

"Congratulations, Mr. Schrieber. Your progress is clearly remarkable and, I agree, within 20 years or so, I can see Bates Training introducing their exclusive new breed with considerable fanfare. I'll make sure you get full credit, Hans, if it works out as well as it's looking right now."

Hans Scrieber beamed at the compliments. The project followed exactly his Germanic concepts of efficiency, orderliness, and predictability. This new line made horse breeding seem boring and archaic by comparison with the new challenges.

The three of us then went a short distance to another building looking, like the others, decrepit and neglected on the outside. But inside, it was ultramodern with gleaming white tile walls, stainless steel equipment of all types, and wall-hung plasma computer screens everywhere. The workers we viewed from an observation area through a full glass wall inside were dressed in pressurized suits featuring plastic bubbles over their heads for a fully sterilized environment. In two small cells adjacent to the observation area were two naked slaves, a male and a female, both the epitome of their gender within the human race.

The male was about 6', broad shouldered with a narrow waist, bubble butted, well muscled throughout, and exceptionally well hung. His face was startlingly handsome; his hide was, below his neck, hairless and a beautiful smooth creamy brown. He had bright green eyes, thick jet black curly hair along with a pencil-line beard cut short outlining his rugged jaw, high cheekbones and thin but full lips. His nose was Grecian and his eyebrows almost met over his wide spaced eyes which were highlighted by long, thick curly eyelashes. His sex was disproportionably large for his body and beautifully shaped, even in the semi-erect state that seemed to be perpetual.

In the cell beside him was a female slave who had exactly the same coloring and basically the same physique with the exceptions her breasts were fulsome and upright with bright pink nipples, her vulva was large with a clitoris that extended a little from her body, even now erect, and she was rounded in her features rather than angular. She too was a beautiful creamy brown.

"They could be twins," Mr. Lindsley observed, obviously excited by what he was looking at.

"Close, Mr. Lindsley," Hans Schrieber explained as he unlocked the cell doors and motioned for the two to step out and assume a full 'body display' position, something they did as if it were habit. "Their DNA patterns are almost identical - as close as any two slaves we could find that also carried all the traits we were looking for in the new 'Bates Best' breed. Essentially, they are two-thirds white blood, one-sixth black, and one-sixth Polynesian to get that beautiful skin tone and smoothness. We searched all over the world until we found these two rarities to serve as our prototypes for each gender we're planning to produce. But they're not really bred like the 'Black Boys' back there. We just use the sperm and eggs they produce to start the process combining a little genetic altering and some RNA recombinant processes. Once we have a fertilized egg doctored up like we want, we put them in an artificial womb that's recently been perfected and, in precisely 275 days, we have another trial pup to check out. All of this is possible just recently since all the human genomes have been mapped. At least that's the way it's been explained to me by our resident veterinary genetic surgeon, who, incidentally, is one of the highest paid people on your payroll, Mr. Bates, according to Mr. Alcorn. We found Dr. Xhou in South Korea where they are way ahead of the rest of the world in this area due to their intensive research using stem cells."

"Yes, I could see where he would come high," I commented. "Veterinary genetics is a promising field but most complex. But, I'm interested, just what genes are you tinkering with? These two prototypes look about as good as slave stock gets to the naked eye."

"I'd have Dr. Xhou answer your questions, but he doesn't speak English. However, I do know he's adding a bit to the gene controlling testosterone for the male products - a little bit more programmed production for even bigger sexual organs, more semen production, and even more muscular definition matched with altering the gene a bit producing estrogen in the males to lower their aggression and give them even smoother skin. That's just an example. Another is he's tinkering with the eye color genes to make their eyes a bright emerald green instead of just green like these slaves and their melatonin gene to give them protection from the sun no matter how long they are out in it. The list goes on and on, but in each case it's not mutating the genetic inheritance in any way, just enhancing it. Basically, this genetic 'drift,' as it is called, is controlled through a series of processes called epigenetics. We're at the cutting edge of technology here and what better area of apply it than in development of a new slave breed? Dr. Xhou claims his products will be human livestock like you have never seen - everything about them will just be a little more distinctive, a little better in meeting the demands of the marketplace, considerably more beautiful in terms of cultural standards of beauty in our culture, and even a little healthier in that their immune systems are being pumped up a bit. And, as he points out, it will be easy enough to change some bodily characteristics, such as eye color, skin tone, and facial features, to meet each cultures' aesthetic definition of beauty. What slaves would be coveted in Korea, for example, would be a little different that what slaves would be most desired in African markets. But the first versions of 'Bates Best' are all designed for American preferences, similar but better than the two prototypes standing before you that form the basis of development."

"How often do you harvest their semen and eggs?"

"Just once a day for the male; every 28 days, of course for the female. In between, they're well exercised and assigned janitorial work around here to keep them fully occupied. We don't let our staff use them sexually, in that their full output is prioritized for the research. And, of course, they can't have sex with each other - a pregnancy would spoil everything and drain the male as well."

"They never leave the building, I take it?" I asked.

"No, there's plenty of test tube scrubbing and polishing and shining to keep them busy right here all day long. If they ever tried to leave, they're outfitted with shock collars which would stop them dead in their tracks the minute they crossed an exit."

I reached toward the female in front of me and squeezed her well-shaped nipples. She smiled at the stimulation and never moved other than thrusting her breast slightly forward to make my manipulations more convenient. I then did the same to the male who gave me the exact same reaction. Both slaves were obviously extremely well trained as well as being genetically perfect.

"Results to date?" I asked Hans Schrieber.

"See for yourself," he answered excitedly as he pointed to the next room, a room also with an observation area separated by a full glass wall from the nursery inside. "But we only have three male pups and two female pups to date. Unfortunately, we lost two products about 150 days into gestation for reasons we still can't figure out. But these five seem to be doing fine so far."

We looked at the five babies placed in two huge cribs: male pups in one; females in the other. They looked absolutely identical within each gender and each one showed all of the characteristics of their prototype except a little exaggerated. Their eyes were a brighter green, their skin even smoother, and their facial features just a little more handsome. Sexual characteristics would have to be judged later after pubescence had occurrence.

"The very first 'Bates Best,'" Hans Schrieber said with great pride.

"Very promising, Hans, from the looks of it. But can these products be mass produced after all the kinks are worked out?" I asked. "The demand will be in the millions every year eventually."

"There's no reason we're aware of yet that would block that, but you'd need a huge factory specifically designed for this type of production to reach those levels, not this little nondescript place," he laughed.

"But those prototypes can't produce much more than a dozen a year or so due to the shortage of eggs."

"True, but its these products in front of you, plus the next batch and the next that will be the prototypes of the future. It won't be long until we have hundreds of prototypes available, all genetically almost identical. And, as soon as we have enough healthy pups on hand to risk it, we're going to start injecting the female prototype with some fertility drugs where she will start producing five or six good eggs a month instead of just one. We're just unwilling to risk any side effects of that right now in the early stages. But, if that works, we're talking about 60 to 70 eggs a year out of each prototype. Multiply that by thousands of prototypes and you can see where production goals could eventually be met."

"Hans, you're a genius," I said. "If all this works, you'll go down in history as one of the world's best scientific inventors, right up there with Edison, Testa, Westinghouse, Salk, and Teller. But, unlike them, I'll make you one of the world's richest men as soon as these 'Bates Best' are marketed. In fact, we might draft up a little royalty agreement the next week or so where you will get a royalty fee on each 'Bates Best' sold. That will make sure you keep your nose to the grindstone although I don't think you're into slave breeding for the money."

"No, Mr. Bates, you're right. It's not the money. I just like the idea of making human livestock to specification. It's a real power trip for me."

"Perfectly understandable," I replied warmly. "Isn't that why all of us enjoy our work so much? Take Brett Alcorn. He's doing the same thing from the environmental side with his beautifully refined training procedures. You're doing it from the physical side. Put the two together, which we will, and it's the future of slavery, Hans."

With that, we parted company. I dropped Mr. Lindsley off at his office and headed back to the manor house with the intention of checking out the brown slave offering me his cream this morning to see if he should be transferred to our traditional breeding operations. Enroute, I called Mr. Alcorn and asked me to fax over the background material on the brown slave.

When I arrived, I studied the report. The slave typically produced over one-fourth cup of "thick" semen with each discharge given eight hours rest before being pumped. That semen had a high count of viable sperm and he was classified as "highly fertile." He had, as he had said, been used by my great-uncle as a cream stud each and every morning for the past five months and had often been called to the old Mr. Bates' bedroom at night for a good fucking where, not infrequently, he would be sucked off my great-uncle for a fresh load of "anti-aging" cream direct from the source. Prior to his purchase a year ago by Bates Training, he had been owned by a mistress who had him fuck her, under her complete direction, two or three times a day.

Perfect, I thought. He not only could produce plenty of viable sperm on command, but knew how to deliver it. His little display this morning proved he had no trouble getting aroused when needed and that he would be totally cooperative in a breeding situation where he would have to produce on command.

I called the brown slave into my bedroom that night where I tested out his seminal discharge for myself with a good milking and then plowed his ass as a test of compliance to an owner's demands. He passed with flying colors and, when I was through using him a full hour later, I told him, based on his excellent performance in my bed, I was transferring him to another place where he would serve me as a breeder stud.

"I'll miss you and that big prick of yours, boy, but you're one lucky slave - I'm sending you to slave heaven for a randy young buck like you."

"I'll be making babies for my master all the time?" he asked hopefully.

"Yes, and with some of the best-looking girl slaves you've ever seen," I replied as I phoned Mr. Alcorn to arrange the transfer. A few minutes later, a station wagon arrived with a kennel cage in the back. The brown slave with the huge equipment was loaded into the cage, waved goodbye with a big smile on his face, and that was the last I ever saw of him for several years.

FIVE YEARS LATER

"Well, the market's all yours now," Mr. Alcorn said. "Your last competitor just announced they're going under."

"You know, Brett, we'll be able to benefit in more ways than one," I replied. "I'm going to offer to buy up all their surplus stock at a steeply discounted price. We'll keep the best for ourselves and dump the others at a special 'discount' sale aimed at first-time owners. Any left over from that we'll just snuff and sell their remains to the hide tanners and dog food manufacturers. No use wasting good slave chow on shoddy goods. Then, after the market settles down, we'll raise prices 5% across the board and, once the howl from that settles down, another 5% the following year."

"We're taking in over 100 million a month now, Mr. Bates. That should put us up in the $1.5 billion area within 18 months, but supply and maintenance costs are edging up a little - about 2%, I'd say. Mainly maintenance, because the influx of bred slaves is offsetting a slight decline in the ones we get from the courts. And those bred slaves take considerably less training to reach standard. By the way, Mr. Bates, slave hide is really catching on. We got a check from the tanner we use for over $60,000 just for last year's input from us - you know, the few that die in training, a few suicides now and then, and the ones we can't sell. If the price keeps climbing, people are going to start raising thick skinned bucks for their hides alone," he laughed.

"By the way, are you still enjoying 'Driver'?" he continued. "He's getting a little long in the tooth as a bed buck I would think, but the last time I saw him over at the manor house, he told me you were still fucking him regularly. I can send over a fresh young replacement that looks just like him any time you want."

"Don't bother, Brett. He still turns me on and he's hard to beat when it comes to rendering up the best fuck in town. Besides, I'm sending him over to the breeding center one afternoon a month to make sure I have a son of his around when the time comes."

TWENTY YEARS LATER

"The special TV show introducing the two new breeds was sensational, Mr. Bates," Brett Alcorn said to his long-time boss. "Mr. Lindsley said everyone is talking about buying one breed of the other the minute they can get their hands on one."

"Well, we held off introduction, as you know, until we had quite an inventory. Nothing like generating a lot of interest and then not being able to meet the demand. First day sales of 'Black Boys' exceeded our most optimistic projections - 170,000 in the first day alone, mainly by the big corporations with long term orders for 1 million over the next three years. They do seem to be perfect for America's industrial needs and the premium price we're charging will be offset by their longevity and endurance under the absolute worst conditions. It's exactly what America needs at this time - livestock that can be worked hard 15 or 16 hours a day, can be quartered with little more than a blanket and a tent over their head in the worst of weather, and will last for at least 30, even 35 years with minimal upkeep and medical expense before they're not worth the feed they consume. There's not a country in the world that can compete with low-cost labor like that available."

"They sent over a 'Bates Best' for a trial run about a year ago to see what I thought," Mr. Alcorn replied. "Best looking boy I've ever seen in all the years I've been in the business and he's the best thing in bed I've ever had."

"That's exactly what they're designed for - if you can afford one. We've priced the first ones at 2.5 million and we've already sold 20,000 of them - almost all we had. Sold just to the very rich, needless to say, who, in my opinion, just want to own a 'Bates Best' as a prestige item as much as bed them down - sort of the new Rolex or Rolls Royce among the smart set. We're going to limit yearly sales to 20,000 a year so that their value holds up through scarcity alone."

"Those brilliant green eyes really set them off as truly unique," Mr. Alcorn replied. "But the whole package just reeks quality. What really sets them off if that they're all alike."

"I was happy Hans Schrieber finally got the credit he deserves. He's on the cover of every magazine in the world as well as a nominee for all the top scientific prizes. Even Dr. Xhou is getting the Nobel Prize in Genetics. That makes our products all the more coveted."

"Mr. Bates. You're a billionaire many times over now, just like I predicted when we first met. And, without pumping up your ego too much, you're probably the most respected person in America right now. After all, you're the first person in the world to market a distinctive slave breed. No wonder the U.N. has invited you to address their general assembly. I think that invitation alone tells you what the whole world is thinking right now.

"Speaking of pumping, Mr. Bates, are you still using old Driver and that jet-black doorman with a ring in the end of his dick? Lord, they must be the oldest slaves in history still getting plugged every night by their master. Won't you let me send you over one of the new 'Bates Best,' at least?"

"I've had a 'Bates Best' on trial for the past two weeks, courtesy of the Breeding Barns. I've given the slave a run for his money, but you know, Brett, they're just too damn perfect for me. I chained him to the front door so my guests would be impressed and brought that old black up here to the bedroom where he and Driver put on quite a show for me every night when I get bored. And, truth be known, I still think Driver takes a fuck better than any slave I've ever had."

"Well, nothing like experience, I guess," Brett Alcorn replied, "That poor boy was practically fucked to death before you ever got your hands on him 25 years ago. The fact he can still bend over a fucking bench, yet alone push himself up and down on your prick is nothing short of a miracle."

"Brett, never underestimate a well trained slave. We can give you credit for that, my man. 'Training that lasts a lifetime' you always claim. Well, Driver's the living proof of that if any slave is."

"You know, Mr. Bates. I liked you when we first met a quarter of a century ago. Now, I like you even better. That's saying something for someone as cranky as me."

"And my respect for you and your training methods have grown with each year I've been running Bates Training. I couldn't do all this without you, Brett. If you look out the front door, you'll see a small token of my appreciation."

Brett Alcorn went to the front door of the manor house while the new doorman, a 'Bates Best,' promptly opened it for him, sinking to his knees in respect as he passed outside. There, in front of him was a shiny new Rolls with the Bates Training Center logo on each front door with chauffeur looking just like Driver did 20 years ago in one of the tightest, most revealing liveries yet designed in a color that exactly matched the car.

"Wonderful, Brett almost squealed in delight. "Mr. Bates, I've always secretly wanted a Rolls for some reason. Thanks. And that chauffeur looks just like your Driver did when we first bought him for Bates Training Center."

"He should, Brett. I told you way back I was sending Driver over the breeding center a few afternoons. Well, it paid off. There's one of the products that goes with the car. I'm giving another one to Mr. Lindsley for his loyalty over the years. I've got three more in reserve that Driver's training now for me."

"Thank you, Brett. We make a great team."

ABOUT THE AUTHOR

Bill Smith is a prolific writer of various fantasy tales about slaves and the huge variety of fictional societies and settings that foster them.

www.ingramcontent.com/pod-product-compliance
Lightning Source LLC
Chambersburg PA
CBHW060815250626
47162CB00005B/1806